THE A

The security of
island was now th
activists – a grou
State in a bloody ... way was
already paved with ... of acts of violence
and at last they were ready for the final stroke . . .

Steve McGarrett, operating from the famous Five-O headquarters, aided by Danny Williams, Chin Ho Kelly and Ben Kokua, was immediately called to investigate. Somehow they had to nip the revolutionary movement in the bud and find its secret arms cache before the whole island erupted in chaos . . .

Other Hawaii Five-O novels published by Star

SERPENTS IN PARADISE

Further action-packed thrillers in
STAR'S TV SUPERCOP SERIES

KOJAK
Requiem for a Cop

KOJAK
Girl in the River

KOJAK
Marked for Murder

CANNON
The Falling Blonde

COLUMBO
The Dean's Death

COLUMBO
A Christmas Killing

and

THE ROCKFORD FILES

THE ANGRY BATTALION

Herbert Harris

A STAR BOOK
published by
W. H. ALLEN

A Star Book
Published in 1976
by W. H. Allen & Co. Ltd.
A division of Howard & Wyndham Ltd.
44, Hill Street, London W1X 8LB

Made and printed in Great Britain by
C. Nicholls & Company Ltd
The Philips Park Press, Manchester M11 4AU

ISBN 0 352 39849 3

INTRODUCTION

This is the Place . . .

These are the Men . . .

Hawaii is one of the most exciting, most sensual, most mysterious, most beautiful places on earth.

Scenically it is a tropical paradise. Climatically the weather is perfect, it is summer all the year round.

The people are a mixture of all the world's races. The blood flowing through most Hawaiians is a blend of many nationalities – Chinese, Japanese, Filipino, Korean, Spanish, Portuguese, French, German, British, American, and many more.

Hawaii became the 50th State of the USA in 1959, the 50th star on the American flag. Up to the end of the last century it was a monarchy with its own colourful kings and queens.

There are more than twenty islands in the Hawaiian group. Only seven are inhabited. The five principal ones are Hawaii, Maui, Oahu, Kauai, and Molokai.

The men of Hawaii Five-O have their headquarters in Honolulu, capital of the island of Oahu, the big, brash, busy nerve-centre of Hawaiian life. More than eighty per cent of Hawaiians live on Oahu, and fifty per cent of those – some 330,000 – live in Honolulu.

Honolulu is a busy, bustling modern city, equal of any big modern city in America or Europe. It attracts planes, ships, tourists, from all corners of the globe. Hawaii Five-O is a special squad of plainclothes crime-fighters. They work with, but independently of, the Honolulu Police Department. They are answerable directly to the Governor of Hawaii himself.

The men of Hawaii Five-O, themselves a polyglot mixture, swing into action whenever criminal elements threaten the fabric of Hawaiian life.

Their work demands undercover secrecy, complete discretion – and force where necessary. It calls for intelligence, fearlessness, specialised training.

Steve McGarrett is the Hawaii Five-O chief.

His right-hand men are Danny Williams, Chin Ho Kelly, and Ben Kokua.

He has a highly efficient girl secretary called Jenny. Frequently he enlists the help of Che Fong, who is the leading member of Five-O's forensic laboratory.

A small group of people dedicated to stamp out the serpents of evil wherever they rear their ugly heads in the Hawaiian paradise.

The motto on the Hawaiian coat-of-arms is: UA MAU KE EA O KA AINA I KA PONO – "the life of the land is perpetuated in righteousness."

The men of Five-O try to keep that proud motto alive.

CHAPTER ONE

The sound of the explosion when it came was like a distant, muffled clap of thunder, reverberating in a prolonged rumble around the Waianae Mountains on the western side of Oahu Island.

Following the explosion a fire broke out quite quickly, and soon the leaping flames had created an orange-red glow in the sky.

The explosion and fire came late in the evening, long after the fiery sun had dropped like a giant coin into the broad slot of the Pacific between Kaena Point and Pokai Bay.

Steve McGarrett, the head of that unique Hawaiian police squad known the world over as Five-O, was on that particular evening in a specially favoured position both to hear the big bang and see the spectacular glow in the sky which followed it.

McGarrett, and Danny Williams, his Number Two in the inimitable crime-busting force, were much closer to the scene of the explosion – just a few miles away – than they would have otherwise have been.

They were visiting Schofield Barracks, where they were guests of an officer of the U.S. 25th Infantry Division, whose headquarters on the western side of Oahu Island is one of the biggest and best-equipped of army posts to be found anywhere in the Hawaiian archipelago or indeed anywhere in America.

Steve and Danny had been shown some recent Vietcong additions to the museum of military weapons for which this army post is well-known, and were nearing the end of their enjoyable visit when the explosion's heavy protracted thud first reached their ears.

Both the guests and their host, Colonel Lawford, had

heard explosions of various kinds in their anything but peaceful careers, so the sound of this one caused no more than a temporary lull in the conversation to begin with.

Steve and Danny caught their first glimpse of the fire between the mountainous slopes of the Kolekole Pass, the gap in the Waianae range through which Japanese planes zoomed early one morning in World War II to rain death and destruction on the U.S. troops still peacefully asleep in the Schofield Barracks dormitories.

"Say, that fire's gained quite a hold, Steve," Danny remarked.

Steve McGarrett and the Colonel, who had been entertaining them that evening in return for Five-O hospitality in Honolulu, joined Danny at the army museum window from which they could obtain the best view.

"Yeah, it looks nasty," Steve agreed, and turned to Colonel Lawford. "What would the bang have been, Colonel? Exercises? Or just plain quarrying?"

"No, Steve, we don't exercise there, and there aren't any quarries at that point either," answered the army man.

"There's a sugar refinery around where the fire is," Danny volunteered, "and sugar sure burns."

"Not exactly at that point," Colonel Lawford corrected, a stickler for locational details as a good army man ought to be. "I'd say that's a little way up the rise above Malakuli Valley, just to the east of Farrington Highway and to the south-west of Mount Kaala. The sugar refinery, Danny, is more towards Waialua."

Danny acknowledged the correction with a smile.

"And what do you figure is on fire, Colonel?" Steve enquired, feeling the first faint stirrings inside him of some new imminent action in which his Department would eventually be involved.

"It's my guess," the army man replied, "that it's the Harrington bungalow."

"A private residence?" Danny asked with a quick swivel of his head.

"That's right," Lawford confirmed, "a big colonial-type bungalow which Milton Harrington built for his wife."

It was Steve's turn now to swing a quick look on their host.

"You mean Milton Harrington the big sugar man?"

Colonel Lawford nodded.

"That's the guy, Steve. He owns the sugar refinery that Danny spoke about a few moments ago – the one which Old Man Harrington opened up on the edge of the Kapaha sugar plantations just before the Hitler War."

"I remember Harrington Senior dying of a heart attack a few years back," Danny put in.

"Yeah," the military man said, "and his son Milton inherited the business. He had to give up living the sweet life in California and come out here to live anything but a sweet life running a sugar refinery."

Colonel Lawford smiled grimly.

"I understand his wife Dorothy has always hated it here. He built that bungalow for her – to her own specifications – just to stop her belly-aching."

"And did it?" Steve smiled back.

"I believe not," Lawford said. "If that's the Harrington home going up in smoke, he'll have to find her some new toy to play with." He peered through the smoke of a cigar he had just lighted. "The fire looks like it's got under way nicely."

Danny said, "The wind sometimes blows off the sea below Kaena Point, and tonight it's blowing kinda more than it should for the leeward side of the island."

Now, against the illuminated sky, the Five-O men could clearly see the vivid sparks and columns of black smoke eddying heavenwards.

Their ears picked up the thin wailing of sirens as fire-tenders and ambulances went racing to the rescue from the Wheeler Field Air Force Base, their own Schofield Barracks, and other neighbouring communities.

Steve had been thoughtful for a long moment. Suddenly he said, as if speaking his thoughts aloud, "But what do you figure the big bang was *before* the fire, Colonel?"

Colonel Lawford's face straightened perceptibly.

"That's a good question, Steve. Milton Harrington's strong anti-Left-wing views make him a little unpopular among the island's lunatic fringe of Marxists and Maoists."

Danny Williams flicked a hard look at his chief.

"Steve," he said evenly, "this is the second time, isn't it?"

The reply came back, "My own thoughts, Danno. You were thinking of Henry Mackeson?"

Danny nodded.

"Say," the military man intervened, "I remember that now! Some crazy guy left a bomb outside Mackeson's private house, didn't he?"

"Some guy or some doll, you can never be sure these days," Steve said drily. "We never did find out who did it, and that kind of thing gets us real mad at Five-O. Luckily nobody got hurt. It wasn't such a big bang anyway."

"But the pattern is the same here," Lawford said, glancing from Steve to Danny. "Is that what you're thinking?"

Danny Williams said, "Henry Mackeson and Milton Harrington are two of the island's top tycoons, and you can count Oahu's merchant-princes on the fingers of your two hands."

Steve clicked two fingers together.

"We met Milton Harrington one night at the Waikiki Biltmore. You remember that, Danno?"

"You're quite right, Steve. It was when the International Longshoremen's and Warehousemen's Union called a press conference to deny rumours – and they *were* only rumours as it turned out – of Communist infiltration into the I.L.W.U."

McGarrett's lips spread in a tight grin.

"Yeah, and they were saying that Harrington is the first to reach for his Winchester when a Red agitator starts to show the whites of his eyes."

"I wouldn't think too badly of him for that," the Colonel said, looking seriously at the tip of his cigar. "These hot-heads can cause real trouble with their kidnappings and hijackings and terror-bombs. It could go 'way beyond the spite-bombing of rich guys' homes. It could spread to the factories."

"And that's a real frightening thought, Colonel," Steve said. "The Hawaiian economy – its prosperity – is founded on sugar and the canning industry. They keep the island's labour force employed."

The Five-O chief turned to give the army officer a long hard stare.

"Take away the means of full employment, Colonel, and you have an army of men idle – dangerously idle – until the holes in the industrial fabric have been plugged."

Colonel Lawford nodded sombrely.

"And in that sort of climate, Colonel," Steve went on, "the seeds of another island revolution can spring into life. Okay? Put some guns in the hands of the men who have been made idle – and who are short of money – and you have another Cuban situation. Right?"

"We just have to keep watching for the signs, Steve," Lawford said. "All of us."

The three men were thoughtful as they stared across the grounds of Schofield Barracks towards the bright wavering glow in the night sky.

CHAPTER TWO

There was no whirling red blister on the roof of the official car carrying Steve and Danny along the four-lane Kamehamea Highway from Schofield Barracks back into the centre of Honolulu.

Danny Williams, at the wheel, was taking it easy. It was pleasant, now and then, to be able to relax, a rare occurrence for the men of Five-O.

Yet all the way home, Steve McGarrett, with his sharpened sixth sense, had felt the same gnawing presentiment which he had felt earlier. . . .

This meant action for the men of Five-O . . . the usual summons from the top man of the "Aloha State," the Fiftieth State of the U.S.A.

It came within hours.

"McGarrett."

"Yes, Governor."

When the Governor's summons came over the telephone, he never had to announce his identity to the Chief of Five-O. That authoritative voice, calm but firmly decisive, was unmistakable.

"I'd like you to come over at once if you're free," the Governor went on. The polite way of putting it, but nobody ever said No to Hawaii's principal citizen. "There's something rather disturbing come up. . . ."

"I'll be right over, sir."

There was no further conversation, no further wastage of time. Within seconds Steve had left his office in the very old Iolani Palace and was on his way to the Governor's office in the very new twentieth-century Capitol building.

There was something overpowering about the ultramodern Capitol, with its legislative chambers cone-shaped, like volcanoes, and the thirty-six massive cement ribs and columns soaring from the main floor.

But if this unique structure was rather formidable, so was the Governor of Hawaii himself, the man responsible for the maintenance of democratic law and order in the whole group of islands in the Hawaiian Archipelago now forming an American State.

Steve was already aware that the Governor had yet another important assignment for the Five-O team or he would not have summoned him to the Capitol so urgently.

He knew, too, that the Governor – installed behind that wide, gleamingly polished desk in front of a wall decorated by both the American Stars and Stripes and the gold circular seal of the ancient Hawaiian monarchy – would not be smiling quite so readily, that the heavy lines of responsibility would seem to be etched slightly more deeply into that fine distinguished face beneath the dignified silvery hair.

And Steve felt, as he had always felt, a tiny flickering of trepidation as he walked across the big glossy office to face the big man behind the big desk.

"Sit down, Steve."

Well, that was reassuring, Steve thought. The Governor only left you standing when he felt displeased about something, and seldom resorted to Christian-names in his more censorious moods.

McGarrett sat in the chair on the opposite side of the desk. Both men, despite the difference of some years, were handsome, smart, clean-cut, impressive, two public servants dedicated to their jobs.

As he did so, the Governor pushed a slip of paper across the desk, a piece of paper of the kind used for taking copies in a typewriter.

"What do you make of that, Steve?"

McGarrett saw that the paper was pale green, that the message on it had been typed unevenly and with a rather worn ribbon. He read:

"The Officers of the Angry Battalion will meet at the usual place on Monday 4th September at 15:00 hours to discuss supply of SC for SKs and other matters."

As McGarrett frowned, the Governor asked him, "Have you come across that name before?"

"Yes, Governor, but I didn't take it seriously," Steve replied slowly. "It reminded me of the name used by a Left-wing revolutionary mob in England, and broken up not so long back by the Special Branch of Scotland Yard."

"You mean the Angry Brigade?"

"Yes, sir," Steve said, looking at the man across the desk with renewed respect and admiration. The Governor's grasp of events in all parts of the world never failed to astonish him.

The Governor went on, "The aim of that movement, according to reports, was the overthrow of the established regime by any means of violence. I believe the police, in the course of their investigations into a number of bomb outrages, discovered a hidden cache of arms."

"I believe that's true, sir."

Looking at the piece of paper again, Steve asked, "How did you come by this, Governor?"

"It was posted anonymously to the Honolulu Police Department."

"And HPD passed it to you?"

"Yes, Steve."

"Too late to do anything about the meeting mentioned," Steve said. "Monday 4th September – that's passed. It was Labour Day, by the way. Rather apt? And, of course, a general holiday, so no excuse for absentees. . . ."

The Governor leaned back in his chair, making a steeple

of his fingers and holding them against his mouth thoughtfully.

McGarrett went on, "I've had an instinctive feeling for some time, sir, that there *are* the early rumblings of a subversive Left-wing movement on this island. The aim being sabotage to begin with and then an armed takeover."

"Anybody who tried that would be crazy," the Governor said, "with the defence forces we have on Oahu."

"Maybe," Steve countered, "but these nuts can create havoc before they're crushed."

"Do you reckon this movement is well advanced?"

"No, sir. There's nothing yet you can put your finger on. There's always the militant Commie around – he's a part of democracy, I guess. One has to assess the precise moment at which the anti-boss-class troublemaker becomes the guy with the cache of guerilla weapons and explosives stashed away under his bed."

"And somebody, I think, assessed that precise point only a short while ago," the Governor commented in his regular, modulated tones.

The lines in McGarrett's forehead became more pronounced. There was a long moment of silence. The chief executive of Five-O waited.

"I'm referring to Eddie Hastings," the Governor went on evenly. "One of the best newspaper reporters ever to leave the *San Francisco Chronicle* for a job on the *Honolulu Advertiser*."

And now Steve McGarrett's lean, resolute face began to reveal the first faint glimmer of comprehension.

The sudden death of Eddie Hastings had been mysterious, to say the least.

The thirty-year-old newspaperman favoured horseback-riding as his major hobby. He had been riding for most of his life, and was an accomplished enough rider for people to say that, with his comparatively short stature and light weight, he could have made an excellent jockey if he had not decided upon a career in journalism.

One afternoon he had gone riding over one of the well-used equestrian trails around the Koko Head Crater, at the south-eastern tip of Oahu Island and less than half-an-hour's run by car from Honolulu's City Centre.

A few hours later they had found his body, battered and bruised, at the foot of a short incline among a cluster of rocky boulders. Some little way away they found his horse, unhurt and unruffled, quietly grazing.

They said that Eddie Hastings had broken his neck, or he might have survived.

The *Advertiser*, giving only moderate coverage to the incident – for newspapers are notoriously modest when reporting the deaths of their own employees – said that Eddie Hastings had met his untimely death by being thrown from a horse in the Koko Head area.

The details of Eddie Hastings' end flashed through Steve McGarrett's mind as he met the steady gaze of the Governor.

"You mean, Governor, that Eddie Hastings was following some kind of lead that could have taken him straight to the people behind the Angry Battalion?"

"I've an uncomfortable feeling that he was, Steve," the Governor went on. "As a matter of fact, he more or less hinted as much to me a few days before the accident which killed him – if it was an accident."

"Just what did he say, Governor?"

The earnest-faced man on the other side of the desk said, "I met Hastings when I attended a Labour Day reception at the Sheraton-Waikiki Hotel. He asked me if I'd ever considered the possibility of a Cuban-style revolution in Hawaii. He was smiling in that rather supercilious way he sometimes had, and I didn't take the suggestion at all seriously. . . .

"Presently, he said, 'Governor, I shall be in a position very soon to give you some gratuitous information.' I said, 'You mean about our revolutionaries?' And Hastings said, 'That's right, but I hate giving anyone only half a story, so you and my editor will have to wait until the picture is complete. But I assure you, Governor,' he said, 'you are going to be rather shocked if I definitely confirm my tentative leads.' And those were the last words Hastings ever spoke to me."

The muscles in McGarrett's jaws rippled momentarily.

"But Eddie Hastings never lived to tell you, sir. Did his editor know anything?"

The governor shook his head.

"None of the details. If he had, he would naturally have consulted us."

"Yeah."

McGarrett referred again to the small sheet of paper the Governor had handed him.

"*. . . . SC for the SK's. . . .*" he muttered, frown-lines biting deep into his forehead.

"Does that convey anything, Steve?"

"I think I know what the SKs stand for, Governor. The I.R.A. used the same term in Ireland. Sabotage Kits."

The Governor nodded. "And so the SC is something wanted for the Sabotage Kits – something somebody is supplying to them. . . ."

There was a pulse suddenly beating in Steve's temples as a flash of inspiration came to him.

"It's occurred to me from time to time, Governor, that if you wanted to create real havoc in Hawaii, you might start by wrecking the main industry, and then put small arms ino the hands of the men made idle."

"The main industry being sugar?"

"Exactly, sir. And sugar forms a ready-made ingredient

for the explosives often used by revolutionaries." He paused. "I don't think I need tell you what they mix with sugar to achieve their big bangs."

The Governor regarded the Five-O man steadily, then said quietly:

"Sodium Chlorate."

McGarrett nodded. "That could be the SC, sir."

The Governor said gravely, "They've got to store these supplies somewhere, Steve ... and the guns. A storehouse of death and destruction."

"Yes, Governor."

The State's leading citizen sat looking for a moment at the small round gold clock on his desk, then, looking up, said:

"Better take another good look at the Hastings riding accident, Steve. Seen against the explosions we've had – the Mackeson one, and now the Harrington affair – plus this message from the Angry Battalion ... it could well have a connection."

McGarrett nodded again.

The man behind the desk continued, "And see if the I.L.W. Union knows anything about Leftie-militants who might be tempted to try something on the Cuban model. Work on it, McGarrett. And don't take too long."

"Sure, Governor."

The Governor stared at the ceiling.

"What was it that Karl Marx said? 'In the revolution, the workers have nothing to lose but their chains – and they have a world to gain.' "

He smiled a brief, bitter smile.

"And what a world, McGarrett!"

Steve smiled grimly. "Yes, sir."

The Five-O man got to his feet, buttoning the jacket of the well-tailored dark suit which was almost the uniform of McGarrett and his men outside the office in the Iolani

Palace. Hawaii's most important official stood up with him.

"*Aloha*, Governor," Steve said. "We won't waste any time on this one."

"Good."

The tall distinguished man behind the big desk watched the back of McGarrett as the latter strode purposefully from the office in the Capitol.

Outwardly, he told himself, Steve McGarrett could pass for the neat, efficient, well-groomed executive of a big business corporation.

But beneath that sartorial smartness was another breed of big businessman – hard, relentless, implacable, fearless, incorruptible. Well, crime was big enough business – and so was the work of suppressing it, the work of Five-O, police squad extraordinary, who had to live up to the Hawaiian motto – "The life of the land is perpetuated in righteousness."

CHAPTER THREE

Long before the bomb wrecked a wing of the Harrington bungalow, a small, delicate Japanese girl named Suzi Hayashi had filtered almost imperceptibly into the stream of Milton Harrington's life.

She was destined to turn the stream into a torrent.

Her entry into his life was not of the girl's doing. Harrington himself had brought it about.

There had been an ulterior motive in developing this intimacy with her – an objective – but this had almost been forgotten, had become submerged as the physical love grew disastrously between them and became overpowering and irresistible.

Before knowing her he had felt free to indulge in the occasional casual affair. These affairs had always been brief and discreet – fleeting associations for the instant relief of pressing physical needs that his wife Dorothy could no longer satisfy.

Dorothy had never known about his sexual dalliances. He had always feared her reactions, for she was a jealously possessive woman whose temper was strangely passionate when you considered how chillingly unresponsive her strong, big-boned body could be.

He felt sure that the paths of himself and Suzi Hayashi would never have crossed if he had not been an old friend of the newspaperman Eddie Hastings.

Eddie's sudden death had been tragic – and mystifying – and it had affected him more than he was able to understand. The fact that Dorothy had never liked him perhaps made him like Eddie more.

His friendship with Eddie Hastings, who was about the

same age as himself, verged on the fraternal. They had been in the same class at college, had graduated together, had developed a deep respect for each other. They had left California to live and work in Hawaii at very nearly the same time.

Almost fortuitously Milton Harrington had met the journalist only a matter of hours before the accident which robbed the *Honolulu Advertiser* of its finest reporter.

Harrington had been enjoying a long, cool drink on the *lanai*, or outdoor terrace, of the Halekulani, or Waikiki Beach, one of Honolulu's most popular hotels, with its ranch-style architecture and glorious views across Diamond Head, the extinct volcano which had become a beauty-spot.

Glancing to his right, he had spotted Eddie Hastings sitting a few yards away with a girl. Eddie had caught his glance and waved him over with his hand, and Harrington went across to join them.

The girl could have passed at first glance as one of the island's two-hundred-thousand Japanese, but there was a lack of that graceful delicacy, that submissive gentleness one found in most of the purely Japanese girls.

She was much more likely to be of Korean stock, Harrington told himself – bigger, heavier, more muscularly solid, less inclined to smile.

A strange alliance for the journalist, Harrington thought, for Eddie Hastings was a man of small, slight stature, and one could picture him being almost smothered by this amazon of a girl if he ever took her to bed. Was that likely, though? The girl looked more of a lesbian than a man-eater.

"This is a friend of mine – a big sugar tycoon – Milton Harrington," Hastings had said to her, introducing them. "And this is Miki Shibata. . . ." – he had grinned in his derisive way – ". . . about whom I shall say little until you have read her life story in the *Advertiser* . . . assuming I get her life story. . . ."

The girl had forced a faint smile, but it was a cold smile. It went perfectly with the hard, embittered face.

"Eddie is forever romancing," she said.

"Don't misinterpret that remark, Harrington," Eddie had put in with a grimace. "It might suggest that I'm trying to lay her. But God help me if I ever try it. She is bigger than I am, and she is half Korean – the Koreans are masters of self-defence."

Harrington congratulated himself on his accurate assessment.

"So you're Korean?"

"Only half," she answered, her mouth sullen. "Eddie is romancing again. I am half Japanese."

Hastings had said, "It's her sister Suzi who is all Japanese. More gentle. Such a difference!"

The newspaperman – who had always enjoyed banter – seemed to like teasing her, perhaps because she seemed to lack a sense of humour.

"Miki here is like an Olympic wrestler. Her sister Suzi is as fragile as Japanese pottery. You've *got* to meet her sometime, Harrington. She would be right up your street, I think."

"In that case, I'd like to," Harrington answered, wishing he had the gift of smart repartee; he had never been good at duelling with words.

"Okay. You just go along to the Lomilomi, on Maunakea Street, and Suzi will make you very welcome, I'm sure. You know what the Hawaiian word 'Lomilomi' means, of course?"

Hastings had switched the teasing from the girl to himself, Harrington thought, a trifle uncomfortably. The *malihini* – or stranger to the islands, by contrast with the *kama-*

aina – or one actually born in the islands, was often meeting the challenge of the Hawaiian tongue. Harrington had never been very good at it, whereas Hastings, whose profession was words, had managed to master this melodious and mellifluous language.

"Lomilomi? I'm afraid I've forgotten, old man."

"Massage," Hastings had obliged, smirking a little. "Miki's sister – Suzi Hayashi – who is all Japanese and all girl, let me tell you, is the number one masseuse at the Lomilomi massage-parlour on Maunakea Street."

A quick glance was fired by the journalist in the direction of Miki Shibata.

"Miki doesn't like me to talk about her sister . . . her half-sister really . . . do you, Miki? A masseuse is decadent, an unfortunate manifestation of the dissolute and effete Western Capitalist system. That's what you think, isn't it, Miki?"

"Oh, for God's sake shut up," the Korean-Japanese girl had said, a distinctly sharp edge to her rather low-pitched voice.

Milton Harrington had not failed to notice the expression in the girl's eyes as she had thrown a quick look at him.

Embarrassment? No, not exactly that. Nervous apprehension? Fear, even? A little of all these things, Harrington had thought.

"But Suzi's job *is* dreadfully decadent, isn't it, sweetheart?" – Hastings was sniping at the girl again, making her sullen mouth close even more tightly.

Hastings had smiled at Harrington.

"Miki herself works at the Paradise Garden of Rest and Remembrance. Which, by the way, is an extremely capitalistic and acquisitive private cemetery near Makapuu Lighthouse, out on the eastern tip of the island, on Route 72. Maybe you know it?"

A shake of the head from the sugar man.

"You should reserve a plot there, Harrington, for your last resting-place. It's costly but a beautiful place in which to be buried. . . ."

"Do you *have* to keep on?" Miki demanded. One of her hands – large hands – was gripping the other.

But Hastings pressed on, tormenting her.

"Joseph Vladicek, the Superintendent, really puts everything he's got into a burial, old boy – and, like Miki, Miss Tombstone 1973, is really wedded to his work. Miki's his Number One girl – am I right, love? People are dying to have Miki tend their last resting-places. . . ."

Miki Shibata got up suddenly. She had clearly had enough, and wanted to put an end to the conversation.

"Are you coming, then?" she flung at Hastings.

"Yes, of course, my little *ipo*." The Hawaiian word for sweetheart. Hastings had abandoned his chair with a slow, languorous movement. A lazy smile curved his supercilious mouth.

Harrington had always admired Hastings when he was serious; he was not so certain he admired the journalist's more facetious moods.

The man was a brilliant journalist, certainly, tireless and relentless in his digging for facts, fearless in his pursuits of truth and justice and the exposure of corruption.

Perhaps the cynical air of this small, slight man was due to his feeling, deep down inside, that corruption was indestructible and mankind intrinsically rotten. A destroyer of illusions, yes, but a man of unimpeachable integrity. A man to hate and to love.

"You've got to get your jodhpurs on, haven't you, darling?" Hastings was saying to the girl.

Harrington thought he saw anger in the oblique eyes under the long eyelids, in the broad nostrils. The girl was too heavily built for his taste, reminding him of Dorothy.

He was drawn now towards the small and delicate and fragile. . . .

"So you're going riding together?" Harrington had prompted.

And Hastings had nodded affirmation. "That's right. I didn't know until yesterday that Miki was as keen on horse-riding as I am. We're going for a gallop around Koko Head."

"She might even be able to teach you something," Harrington had bantered, catching the journalist's mood.

"I think Miki can teach me a lot . . . an awful lot," Hastings had answered.

Thinking about Hastings' remark afterwards, Harrington realised that there was some special significance about it, some hidden meaning, some disguised hint. But Eddie Hastings had often baffled his listeners with cryptic comments.

"I can tell before ever we start riding," Hastings had continued jokingly – glancing down at the girl's broad, ample buttocks – "that Miki has a good seat."

He had then playfully slapped her behind, and Miki Shibata hadn't quite liked that, Harrington felt. Her eyes and her thick broad lips had looked churlish and resentful.

"*Aloha!*" Hastings had said with a wave of his hand.

"*Aloha!*" Harrington had responded.

That conversation was the last he had ever had with the newspaperman.

*

So there were two reasons why Milton Harrington eventually found his way to the Lomilomi massage-parlour on Maunakea Street.

The first to satisfy his mind, the second to satisfy his body.

He could not believe that Eddie Hastings' fatal horse-riding accident was completely credible. Hastings was much too good an equestrian. He knew how to avoid accidents; better still, he knew how to fall. Good riders did not sustain such injuries as Eddie Hastings was said to have suffered.

And that girl. The one who clearly despised the "dolce vita" aspects of "decadent Western Capitalism," and yet was quite happy to work for a private burial-ground which made capital out of the dead and those who mourned them....

What of her?

He experienced a nagging desire to talk to her. She was a leading player in a mystery, and Harrington was irritated by unsolved mysteries.

She couldn't have been Eddie Hastings' mistress; she was clearly not feminine enough for that. A platonic friend, then? And yet her personality, her outlook, had nothing in common with the journalist's.

So why had Hastings cultivated her?

Come to think of it, Hastings very seldom cultivated people for pure friendship; it was nearly always to pick their brains. Harrington's own friendship with the newspaperman was a rare thing, a precious thing, a coming together of like minds.

That girl.... Why?

Yes, he had to see her again, to ask questions. He had no idea what sort of questions.

So he went first to the Paradise Garden of Rest and Remembrance. He knew he would not want to stay long in the place. The headstones would be ostentatious, and beneath them would be ostentatious coffins. Supreme examples of the high cost of dying, and not the nicest example of the private-enterprise world to which he himself belonged. But perhaps it had its place in a crazy world....

He had expected to talk to Miki Shibata first, since she was apparently "Number Two" to the Superintendent. Instead, to his surprise, it was Number One himself, the Superintendent, who greeted him.

"Can I help you, sir? My name is Joseph Vladicek."

A tall man, broad-shouldered, with a large head and thick blond hair. His rather flat features helped to emphasize his Slav origins.

In Hawaii – where the population of three-quarters-of-a-million represented a greater mixture of races than you could find perhaps anywhere on earth – one did not usually quiz people on their racial background.

But Harrington found himself asking, "Russian?"

A pause. Then: "No, sir, Hungarian actually." The big blond man quite obviously didn't trust him, Harrington thought, and seemed slightly nervous. He wondered why.

Vladicek suddenly became the professional mortician.

"You have lost a relative, sir? Or perhaps you wish to discuss a family burial plot. . . .?"

Harrington smiled politely. "Neither, I'm afraid. I should like to have a word with Miss Miki Shibata if she's here."

"Oh, I see. A . . . social call." The man was evidently still dubious. "I'll see if she's around. . . ."

The words had hardly left his lips when the girl suddenly appeared at the door of the office.

She looked at Harrington hard for a moment. Then, without any sort of cordiality, she said, "Mr. Harrington, isn't it? – the sugar king?"

Full marks for memory and observation, he thought.

"Not *the* king – there are several Hawaiian sugar kings, most of them more important than I am."

She didn't return his smile, but said laconically, "You wanted to talk to me?"

"Well, yes...." Her hard stare was disconcerting. "About my friend Eddie Hastings...."

She said unemotionally, "The unfortunate accident – that was very sad."

"Yes, very," Harrington answered. "I can't believe it happened."

"What do you think happened?"

"I don't know," he said. "Quite frankly, I find the whole thing rather mystifying."

"So do I, Mr. Harrington."

"What were the circumstances exactly, Miss Shibata? There was not very much detail in the newspaper report...."

He watched her face, but it told him nothing. It was a face without expression. But the face of the man Joseph Vladicek was also stony. However, he told himself reasonably, morticians and cemetery-keepers were not expected to be lively, animated people, were they?

"I'm afraid I don't know what happened," she replied.

Harrington raised his eyebrows. "Oh.... I was under the impression that you were with him?"

"No," said Miki Shibata in a flat monotone, "we had separated, gone our different ways. Mr. Hastings was alone when he met with his accident."

"You mean ... you left him to return home?" He carefully watched her face.

After a slight hesitation, she said, "We had quarrelled, you see. I'm afraid I can't tell you what about. It is ... personal."

"Well, I've no wish to be inquisitive," Harrington said with a slight edge to his voice. "It's just that I ... I was quite a good friend of Eddie's, and I thought I ought to know just what ... just what happened at the finish. You understand?"

"Well, I'm sorry I can't tell you anything, Mr. Harrington." She glanced pointedly at her wristwatch. "Was that all you wanted to ask me? I have some rather important things to discuss with Mr. Vladicek."

"Yes . . . yes, of course."

Outside, in the cooling east trade winds blowing across Oahu's easternmost point, Harrington paused briefly to look at the neat, well-kept ranks of graves and headstones stretching away into the distance.

In the cloying, almost sinister silence, only the mocking screams of some seabirds attempted to shatter the last long sleep of those privileged dead who lay in "Paradise".

Or could it be the dead themselves, spurred on by the departed Eddie, screaming out: "She's lying! She's lying!"

*

And so – as a last resort – to the "Lomilomi," a few degrees higher in respectability, Harrington thought, than some of the massage-parlours which had sprouted, alongside the blue-movie houses and clip-joints, in the sleazy downtown area of Honolulu sometimes compared with Soho or Chinatown.

Incongruously, it was only a few blocks westward – or "*ewa,*" as you say in Hawaii – of the Iolani Palace, in which the Five-O men had their headquarters; and the State Capitol, in which the Governor had his office; and Washington Place, the Governor's official residence.

Unanswered questions were still nibbling away at Harrington's mind, questions that Miki Shibata would never be likely to answer directly. Maybe Eddie Hastings had tried to make her. . . .?

That was one reason for going to the "Lomilomi."

The other reason was to find out if Hastings had been correct in his assessment of Suzi Hayashi, Miki's half-sister.

All Japanese . . . and all girl. . . .

Dorothy, his wife, had never been all girl, or all woman.

Until recently, the pressures of running the refinery had helped him to sublimate the urgent demands of his body. But recently. . . .

He had been once to a massage-parlour, and the male masseur there, he thought, must have been training as a sumo-wrestler and building up his own muscles at the expense of Harrington's.

But with a masseuse like Suzi Hayashi, the whole concept of massage was different.

Her soft, cool fingers had stroked gently, caressingly over his flesh with the lightness of moth's wings, and his body had stirred like an imprisoned bird beneath the towel across his loins.

Suzi was totally different from her half-sister Miki. Long, shiny, silky hair, black as liquorice, framed a sweet oval face, a face of amber porcelain, the skin as smooth as flower petals, her almond-shaped eyes the colour of black plums.

She was like a pastel painting, he thought, a tiny figure, immaterial and sprite-like.

Feeling her fingers moving across his thickening body had provided Harrington with the most beautiful moments of his life.

He realised what the Japanese businessman derived from the attentions of their geisha girls, the little humming-bird women who managed to make sensual things spiritual. He could have kicked himself for never having discovered the Lomilomi before.

He had gone back to the massage-parlour again and again, and one day he had given her a lift home in his car.

"It's raining," he said, and they walked, or half ran, to the car parked a few hundred yards away.

The rain was unusual and fortuitous. It hardly ever rains in Hawaii, where there are no sharply contrasting seasons, where it is blue, balmy summer all the year round. But this was a shower – a short, sharp, sudden shower, Hawaii's "liquid sunshine".

As Suzi Hayashi snuggled comfortably beside him in the cream Cadillac convertible, he found himself vaguely intoxicated by her perfume, the heavenly pikake-jasmine she seemed to favour. This time even the smell of her wet plastic macintosh gave him a sensual pleasure that made him want to touch her.

Harrington was not unused to Japanese people. There was an abundance of them in Hawaii. Quite a few were employed at the refinery. But somehow Suzi Hayashi was different . . . so very different.

At times when the pressure of business problems weighed heavily on him, Milton Harrington allowed his mind to drift momentarily to the simple pleasures he found with the Japanese girl, the details of their first encounter, their first talk over the tiny white saucers of *saké*, Japanese rice-wine, which she had handed to him almost ritualistically.

From the massage-parlour in Maunakea Street, with its evocative oriental decor, to the girl's small and not very lush apartment on River Street, near Honolulu Harbour, was not very far, and Harrington found himself wishing it were further on that first exciting journey in that rare and strangely propitious shower of Hawaiian rain.

To his utter joy, she had said, "You would like to see my room?"

What man with warm blood in his veins could have said "No"?

And, anyway, what loyalty did he owe to his wife Dorothy? On those rare occasions when she lent him the use of her flesh, she did it merely as a marital duty. What right had she to demand his fidelity. . . .?

That was how it had begun. And soon Harrington had almost forgotten his reason for going to the Lomilomi, the mystery of Eddie Hastings' death, the strange ambiance of sinister venom around "Miss Tombstone," as Eddie had jokingly called her.

His head was full of Suzi now. He knew he had become absurdly – divinely – in love with her, and the madness was shutting out everything except his recurring vision of the inevitable fusion of their bodies.

She had said, "The god Inari is said to bring rich lovers to the girls who offer up prayers to him. I did that, and he brought me you."

Her small china-doll face, which had been full of strange melancholy a moment before, was now a puckish face, gay and laughing.

She liked to put on a kimono for him, a *yukata* which could serve as negligee or bath-wrap or even nightgown; a dazzling affair in gold and blue embroidered with big cherry-blossoms and dragons.

She would squat on a cushion on the floor, fingering the turquoise *obi* or sash, gazing up at him and chattering away.

At first Harrington had just watched her, desiring her.

Then had come the moment when he had said, "I could very easily fall in love with you. . . ."

Not just "could," he thought; it had already happened, hadn't it?

"But you know nothing about me," she said, sitting very still with her soft cat-like eyes on him; a painting, an oriental painting. . . .

"I've met your sister."

"Miki Shibata? My half-sister actually."

"Okay, your half-sister."

"Her father was my mother's first husband – a Korean. He was a Communist and was killed when he fought for North Korea against the South. Miki was just a small girl then. My mother married again soon after – this time a Japanese like herself – a businessman like you, but not such a rich one."

Unexpectedly, she was telling him everything, all he had hoped to find out. He had not had to ask, after all. Perhaps now he didn't even want to know. He wanted just the girl, the sweet physical happiness she could bring him, not her family dossier.

But Suzi seemed to like talking, and her soft, singing voice was all a part of her sensual charm, making him want to listen.

"Miki is the clever one. Very brainy. Always reading books, newspapers, anything she could lay her hands on. Her brain is very good, far better than mine. . . ."

As if that really mattered, Harrington thought. Dorothy had a good brain. At times she had been able to stimulate him mentally. Never physically.

"My father was going to send Micki to university. And then he died suddenly, and there was no money. Creditors took most of it."

Things became clearer. It would account for Miki's Leftist leanings, wouldn't it? A father killed fighting for the Communist cause. Then being deprived of a promised university education when her mother became one of the unlucky have-nots. Yes, it figured. His reasoning was not particularly tinged with pity, however. Milton Harrington was a rock-hard realist; there was little room for maudlin sentiment in his make-up.

"All the same, Miki made a career for herself," Suzi had continued. "She has a very good job."

"Yes," Harrington had said, "I know what she does."

The small oval face had become curious.

"How did you meet my sister?"

"She was with a good friend of mine," he answered truthfully. "A newspaperman named Eddie Hastings. Did you know him?"

Suzi was nodding her head.

"Only slightly.... I knew that he was chasing my sister."

"Chasing?"

"Well, wasn't he?"

"Probably. I don't really know."

Then, with a wistful look on her face: "She would have done better to marry somebody like Eddie Hastings. I mean ... why did she have to pass up such a chance for a man like Pedro Mindoro?"

She had awakened fresh interest in him. "Pedro Mindoro?"

"A Filipino. A labourer who works only with his hands. He is completely illiterate. Handsome, I suppose, and virile, but without any education. How could a girl with a brain like Miki's get herself involved with a man like that?"

Harrington had frowned in puzzlement.

How indeed? How did you equate a girl who looked like a lesbian with a handsome virile Filipino lover? Or a heavy reader with one who was illiterate? What sort of alliance was that?

"Mindoro is a bad egg, I can feel it," Suzi was saying. "I just don't understand Miki. She has a brain as big as her body. She is big all over."

It had brought a smile to his mouth. "Yes, I know."

"I wish I had brains. Still, I'm very good with my hands. I suppose that's why I make a good masseuse, being so good with my hands?"

He realised later that he should have asked her more

about Miki's strange association with Pedro Mindoro; why Mindoro was a "bad egg." But at the moment, watching her hungrily, he knew that the information he had come for was the last thing he now wanted. He wanted only to touch her, to hold her.

And presently she had come across to where he sat on the *punee*, the Hawaiian style studio-couch, the lounging kimono gaping open at her neck, revealing her small firm breasts like lotus-buds.

She had moved against him freely, spontaneously, with a sleepy smile, and the kimono had slid away from her with an exquisite slowness.

Then she was holding him in an embrace astonishingly strong for such a small, seemingly frail girl.

Before their mouths joined, she fastened her small white teeth, like an animal, on one of his lips. And then in the unrestrained enfolding of their bodies, the sweet mingling of their breath, Harrington had forgotten the ugly, menacing world that lay outside the small, humble apartment that was on Honolulu's River Street.

It filled him with a warm pride. He must be almost twice her age, he thought. If only it were possible to tell Dorothy about it, to make her realise that other women – younger women – desired him as a lover, even if she didn't.

They lay together a long time.

An Hawaiian had once said to him: "The *punee* couch is not made to sit on, but to lie on. The *hikiee* couch is wider, and better for two."

But the *punee* was quite adequate.

Would he ever be curious again about her background? Would he ever again concern himself about her sister, about her sister's "bad egg" boyfriend?

Did it really matter now about Miki Shibata, and Pedro Mindoro, and all the other Lefties who had engaged Eddie Hastings' attention? – the faceless ones who threatened

Harrington's way of life and whom he had pledged himself to root out and destroy?

"Yes," he had murmured softly against her mouth, "you are wonderful with your hands." But even as they made love his conscience was still faintly troubled. . . .

*

On his increasingly more frequent visits to her apartment, Harrington saw her naked often enough, and yet each time she revealed to him her small delicately-moulded body, the aching desires rose up again in his belly.

"You're the most beautiful girl I ever saw," he told her, coming up close to her as she stood before her dressing-table mirror. He folded his arms around her from behind, holding her small breasts like two warm throbbing birds cupped in his large strong hands.

She said, smiling at him across her shoulder, "I have to dress. I'm going to the temple."

"The temple?"

"Yes, I told you I would be going, but you were not listening. Would you like to come?"

She donned a thin white blouse, sleek as her own skin. It had a transparency that allowed the pale amber of her body to shine through it.

"What sort of temple?" he asked vaguely. He would have much preferred to make love again.

Suzi answered, "A Buddhist temple. There are temples all over Hawaii for Japanese and Chinese and Koreans."

"Yes, of course, I should have realised what you meant. But it's difficult to think of you as Japanese . . . as a Buddhist . . . as a worshipper at a temple. . . ."

"You think I am too wicked to worship at temples?"

Harrington smiled at her indulgently, and said, "I don't know."

She said, with a childish simplicity, "I suppose I'm not a good girl . . . not virtuous, I mean. But I'm not as wicked as my sister. She is bad, deep down, despite her cleverness."

Oh God, he thought, she had dragged him back to the mundane – the good, the bad, the virtuous, the wicked. It was better to drink the heady wine of physical love, and thus shut out the world. . . .

"Does your sister worship Buddha too?"

Suzi said scoffingly, "Far from it! She is an atheist. Sometimes I am worried about her."

"Worried?"

"She is mixed up with bad people."

Harrington, whose instinct for trouble had always been sharply tuned, was affected by a faint frisson of unease, a presentiment of lurking menace.

So Miki Shibata was mixed up with some bad people.

Eddie Hastings had cultivated her company for no apparent reason, unless it were to use her as a guide to where he wanted to go.

And Eddie Hastings had died suddenly, in an inexplicable way. . . .

Harrington asked carefully, "You mean she's mixed up with criminals?"

Suzi said uncertainly, "I'm not sure." She stood for a moment gazing thoughtfully from the window, across the Nuuanu Stream bordering River Street to where some old houses, former brothels, were being bulldozed to make way for modern buildings.

"I told you about Pedro Mindoro . . . the Filipino . . . the one who can't read or write . . . the one she sleeps with. . . ."

"Yes." (Sleeps with? Harrington wondered.)

"He is only one of them."

"You mean there's a gang?"

Her brow creased and her eyes were troubled.

"I think so . . . well, kind of. . . ."

"What makes you say that?"

"I've looked in her handbag. I've seen messages."

"Messages?"

She hesitated for a moment, then went to her own handbag. She took from it a folded sheet of paper and brought it across to him.

"I took this from Miki's bag," she said a little shamefacedly. "I thought I ought to ask you about it, because you would know more about these things than I do. I've not shown it to anyone else. It puzzled me a lot. . . . I would like to know what you think it means. . . ."

Harrington opened out the sheet of paper. He saw it contained only a short message, typewritten on flimsy green copy-paper, the type rather uneven and faint.

"*The Officers of the Angry Battalion will meet at the usual place on Monday 4th September at 15:00 hours to discuss supply of SC for SKs and other matters.*"

Harrington suddenly felt cold, as if the ghost of Eddie Hastings were hovering at his side, reading across his shoulder.

He said, "Does your sister know you have this?"

Suzi shrugged. "She probably guesses. Miki knows I'm curious about her. But I don't like the sound of it, do you?"

"No," Harrington answered slowly, still studying the short message through narrowed eyes. "May I keep it for a while? I would like to think about this a bit longer, Suzi. It might be a good idea to contact some . . . some friends."

The Japanese girl, her expression partly perturbed and partly confused, said, "I don't want to get Miki into trouble, you understand. I just want to try and help her, because I think she has got in with the wrong people."

"Yes," he said consolingly, "yes, of course. We can try to help her together."

Harrington refolded the sheet of paper, put it carefully inside his wallet, and then was suddenly smiling at her again.

Hell, he thought, that goddam piece of paper had momentarily dragged him out of his small paradise again. He wanted to struggle back into it. . . .

"Now, about this temple," he said cheerfully. "You said you would show it to me." (Anything, anything, to stay with her a little longer, to avoid the clamouring demands of his troubled world and troubled conscience.)

"You would like to come with me now?"

"Yes, I'd love to."

The temple was only a few blocks from the City Centre, and with its curved and pointed roofs and red-painted skeleton-like post-and-lintel gateway was a tiny microcosm of a more ancient and mysterious world.

When they were outside, she touched his arm, that mere touch thrilling him in the most exotic way.

"You have some socks on?" she asked, a question so inconsequential and puzzling that Harrington smiled.

"Socks?"

"Nobody ever enters the sanctuary of this temple without first removing his shoes," Miki told him, her small face quite earnest. "There are some small felt slippers if you want them, but your socks will do."

"Yes," Harrington said, "I have socks on. I'd quite forgotten that one has to enter barefooted. The highly polished floor would be pretty cold, I guess, for bare feet."

"The removal of the shoes is not just to keep the beautiful floors nice," Miki said seriously. "It is also out of respect for our Gautama Buddha."

"Yes, of course," Harrington said in a chastened voice.

The sanctuary of the temple, smaller than he had thought, had pews of pungent sandalwood, and sitting facing them the fat, smiling, cross-legged Gautama, father of Buddhism, in shiny metal.

"A copy of the great bronze Buddha at Kamakura in Japan," she whispered reverently. "The small wooden chests you see contain the spirits of the gods."

The temple was empty, save for the two of them, and the heavy Buddhist symbolism somehow depressed him. She was quite solemn during their stay, and he realised that whatever her morals might be, she had been brought up to respect Buddhism's ritual and solemnity.

"The basis of our true belief is Shintosim," she said, still whispering. "One of its ancient teachings is loyalty to the State."

"That's pretty worthy," Harrington whispered back.

"Miki thinks it's a thing of the past."

Yes, Harrington thought to himself, she would, she would. . . .

The atmosphere of the place had become uncomfortable, sinister, wrapping itself around him like icy fingers. His feet, without shoes, had grown cold.

He shivered slightly and said, "Now that I've paid my respects to your gods, may I go outside and get warmed up again in the sun?"

"Sun worship is also a part of Shintoism," she told him.

Suzi bowed low before the figure of Buddha before following him out.

It was not until he arrived back home that Harrington thought again about the mysterious piece of paper which Suzi had handed to him.

He took it from his wallet and re-examined it.

It meant nothing to him, nothing at all, but the term "Angry Battalion" and the fact that it was so cryptic caused him uneasiness.

He realised that if he took it to the Honolulu Police he

would be implicating himself. He would have to explain how he came by it.

His illicit association with the little masseuse at the Lomilomi would be dragged into the harsh light of publicity, talked about in the country clubs and on the golf-courses.

He would probably expose Suzi Hayashi to danger by revealing that she had passed the note on to him. He found it horrifying to think of any harm coming to her.

He owed it to himself and to Suzi to avoid incriminating either of them.

But Eddie Hastings. . . .

He owed something to Eddie also. . . .

At length, after a great deal of agonising soul-searching, Harrington put the piece of paper in an envelope, without any covering note, and addressed it to the Honolulu Police Department.

It was through this strange sequence of events that the telltale piece of paper eventually reached the men of Hawaii Five-O.

If the action of posting off that scrap of paper to the authorities did something to alleviate Harrington's conscience, it did scarcely anything to reduce his feeling of uneasiness.

However, his feelings of doubt and insecurity would have been infinitely worse if he had known that he was being kept under surveillance.

The sugar man was at present blissfully ignorant of the fact, but his meetings with Suzi Hayashi had been carefully watched and certain conclusions drawn.

His movements had been watched by two different people with quite different objectives.

CHAPTER FOUR

When Steve McGarrett visited the headquarters of the I.L.W.U., he took along the newest recruit to the Five-O squad, Ben Kokua.

The good-looking Ben – a *kamaaina*, or true Hawaiian, like his popular predecessor in the Five-O team, Kono – had never been inside the I.L.W.U. building, and Steve thought he ought to see it to complete his knowledge of Honolulu.

The I.L.W.U. – the controversial International Longshoremen's and Warehousemen's Union – had commissioned a Mexican painter, Pablo O'Higgins, to decorate the place with a great mural, taking up two floors of the staircase, depicting the story of labour in Hawaii – from the days when the tough *lunas*, the plantation overseers, spurred the men to work harder with cracks of a whip, to the modern enlightened age of democratic trade unionism.

"There's no better fresco than that anywhere in the Soviet bloc," Steve had grinned. "But the I.L.W.U. has done a very good job in Hawaii, Ben, and everyone here respects it."

To the man who received them – courteously, efficiently, co-operatively – and motioned them to chairs on the other side of his desk, Steve said:

"I intend to come straight to the point, Mr. Williamson. Have you any knowledge of any dangerous 'subversives' in the I.L.W.U. movement?"

The man facing them answered this opening gambit with another question.

"Mr. McGarrett, would you remember the work of the late Jack Hall?"

"He was slightly before my time," Steve replied, smiling, "but I do know a little about him."

"Sure you do, Mr. McGarrett, and who doesn't? He organised a lot of important strikes and was astute enough to win them. He scored a great victory – through the best of public relations – in that early disastrous Sugar Strike of 1958, and he forced management to give a 23 cent an hour increase after management had told him that the 25 cents increase he'd asked for was completely out of the question. You don't remember that?"

"Not all the details," Steve admitted.

"I'm just mentioning these facts as a preliminary to saying that there have been very good labour-management relations in this State ever since. But for Jack Hall and the I.L.W.U., there could have been plenty of real trouble over the past dozen years or so. That's well worth remembering."

"I've never questioned that, Mr. Williamson. The Union has done a great job. I think everyone here recognises that – the bosses as well as the workers."

The man on the other side of the desk broke into a warm, friendly smile, and sat back with his hands folded across his stomach.

"Well, that's fine, Mr. McGarrett. And having got that bit of trumpet-blowing out of the way, let's get down to brass tacks and consider your question." He pursed his lips. "Do I know of any workers who are likely to be troublemakers on the grand scale. . . . ?"

Steve waited, his eyebrows raised questioningly.

"Yes, Mr. McGarrett. The Union has to keep its ears to the ground just as you fellows do up there in Five-O. And I'm going to pass on a small piece of information that may or may not mean anything."

"The smallest scraps of information are always useful,"

answered the Five-O chief, "and, of course, will be treated in the strictest confidence."

"It'd better be," Williamson said with an uncertain smile. "I take it that you've come to me as part of a general investigation into some underground subversive movement against the State of Hawaii?"

McGarrett inclined his head and said, "Perhaps you'll keep *that* under *your* hat."

"Oh, sure," the Union spokesman said. "Any work you do in that direction will win the full support of the Union. We don't want any part of any group aspiring to bloody revolution. We've had our revolts in these islands and we don't want them again. That's why I'm going to give you a tip-off, Mr. McGarrett. I think it's my duty to do that – my duty to the State and to the Union."

Steve nodded. Williamson sat looking down at the top of his desk for a moment, then looked up.

"There's a man called Pedro Mindoro."

"Get that down, Ben," Steve said crisply.

Ben began to scribble in a notebook.

"Spanish-Hawaiian?" Steve prompted.

"He says Filipino. He's a longshoreman, loading and unloading exports and imports for White Cross Mercantile, the shipping outfit. He used to work for another shipping crowd – Mackeson's."

"Henry Mackeson?"

"Yeah. Mackeson fired him when he was found distributing Commie leaflets among the other workers. . . . 'Take Up Arms For Freedom' . . . that kind of crap . . . you know the kind of thing."

Steve drew his brows together.

"And then somebody left a bomb outside Mackeson's private house. . . ."

"That's right. I guess Mindoro had an alibi at that time?"

"Yeah, he would."

"I'm not making any accusations, Mr. McGarrett. You had nothing to go on then, and have even less to go on now. What's more, I don't think such an action on the part of Mindoro – if, in fact, he did it – would ever be approved by any underground organisation planning a big coup. Such isolated acts of personal spite are too petty to be of any real use to people out to overthrow the Establishment."

"Yeah." Steve frowned again. "Would you know if this guy ever worked for the Harrington refinery?"

Williamson searched his memory. "I'm not sure about that. It's possible. He's moved around quite a bit."

"Never mind. We'll check."

The Union man said, "One has to assume that the bomb at the Harrington bungalow was the work of some guy with a chip on his shoulder. What else? But don't tell me that any revolutionary group with dreams of an island takeover is going to piddle around with bombs planted in doorways."

Steve said, "That's my view too, Mr. Williamson, although it's been done in Ireland and in England. My view is that a disruption of industry is what they'd go for here."

"Is there any imminent danger of that happening?" Williamson asked.

"Let's say there have been ominous signs," Steve told him non-committally, "just signs. But the job of Five-O is to try and put out political forest fires before they start burning."

"In that, Mr. McGarrett, you can rely on our co-operation all the way," the Union spokesman promised him.

Steve and Ben got up, shook the hand of their host, and prepared to leave.

"By the way," Williamson added as an afterthought,

"this guy Pedro Mindoro is illiterate. Can't read or write, they say."

Steve McGarrett commented, with a tight smile, "I guess that accounts for the chip on the shoulder."

The I.L.W.U. man grimaced. "The chip is his head, Mr. McGarrett. I only hope you get him before he uses his chip to start any forest fires."

"We will," Steve promised, "we will."

CHAPTER FIVE

It had been proved time and time again that Chin Ho Kelly, the Five-O operative of the oddly mixed Chinese and Irish parentage, had a specially winning way with the opposite sex.

Any woman who was susceptible to the electric impulses of the male libido would quickly succumb to the quiet, sympathetic charm of Chin Ho Kelly, whose personality somehow blended Chinese good humour with a dash of the Irish blarney.

But within a few seconds of meeting her, Chin Ho had the feeling of having met his Waterloo in the person of Milton Harrington's wife Dorothy.

She was a tall blonde, robustly built but clearly ice-cold. Chin Ho got on best with women who gave off warmth, like a stove. Dorothy Harrington was not like that. But with a little luck, and despite her formidable manner, he hoped she would talk. Most women did in the long run.

Not all the Harrington bungalow had been damaged. Only one wing had suffered. But since the explosion she had moved out of the place and into a private suite at Makaha Inn, the vast hotel and apartment development on the Island's West Coast, not far from the site of the bungalow.

Chin Ho found her sitting beside one of nine man-made lagoons created by a Honolulu millionaire, with a view down a breathtaking valley to the Makaha Beach and its great "combers," the twenty-foot-high surf-riding waves bursting over coral, black lava rock and white sand.

The skimpy deep-yellow bikini that barely covered her showed that Dorothy Harrington, only a little on the right side of forty, still had a good body. Firm breasts, flat belly, no surplus rolls of fat, slim well-shaped legs. Her Hawaiian sun-tan flattered her, emphasising the blueness of her eyes.

Her face was less well-preserved – a little raddled even – perhaps because of the endless succession of highballs, liberally mixed with Bourbon or rye, which nowadays she drank mostly on her own.

Chin Ho Kelly could tell at a glance that Mrs. Harrington was not a happy woman. Her disillusionment and frustration showed up clearly through the hard enamel of her too-heavily lined, too-heavily veined poker face.

She sat alone in a white-painted rattan chair beside a matching table on which stood the inevitable tall, ice-laden highball.

"Please pull up a chair," she said in a rather toneless, languid voice, tinged with weariness. "Would you care for a drink?"

"Thank you, no."

"What did you say your name was?"

"Chin Ho Kelly."

She smiled a humourless, world-weary smile and said, "Quaint."

Her face straightened again suddenly. "Is Five-O any good?"

"We like to think so, Mrs. Harrington. Much depends on the sort of help we get."

She looked away across the feathery *kiave* trees, bending towards the ocean, and stared distractedly at the tremendous creamy-white breakers leaping and curving out of the turquoise and wine-dark Pacific.

After a moment she said, "I don't think I can help you very much, Mr. Kelly. When the time-bomb exploded at the bungalow, I was not there, so I didn't see anything."

"That was very lucky for you, Mrs. Harrington."

"Yes, it was, wasn't it?" She tilted the glass to her lips, a little too scarlet, and swallowed. "So incredibly lucky that I feel sometimes I ought to get down on my knees and pray."

She fumbled in a deep raffia bag and produced a pack of Chesterfield cigarettes. She offered one to Chin Ho, but he shook his head and took out the old-faithful pipe which he always preferred.

She said, in the act of lighting the cigarette and blowing smoke towards the deep blue Hawaiian sky, "The bomb, by the way, was placed immediately outside the room in which I usually sleep."

"You sleep in there alone?"

Dorothy Harrington shot a sharp look at him, and her aggressively red lips parted in a small, sour smile.

"Yes, Mr. Kelly, quite alone . . . regrettably. Meaning that my husband doesn't demand his conjugal rights all that often."

Chin Ho put in uncomfortably, "I was just trying to get clear in my mind if the bomb was intended for both of you or just one of you."

"That's a good question, isn't it, Mr. Kelly?"

She smiled her astringent smile again, and turned to gaze with dull, bored eyes in the direction of the sea.

"But that night you were not sleeping there?" Chin Ho prompted.

"By a lucky chance, no. An old schoolfriend of mine living over at Waianae rang up quite late and said they were throwing a party and would I like to go. I was very bored, so I said Yes, and got the car out. The bomb went off a couple of hours later – when I ought to have been in bed – but I knew nothing about it until I got home in the small hours."

"Your husband was not at home either?"

Another of her forlorn, cynical smiles.

"Milton is hardly ever at home. It's been like that for some little while now."

"Another woman?" Chin Ho asked frankly.

She hesitated for a moment, then: "Yes. Milton has a mistress now. It's the first time he's taken up seriously with one woman. There were probably a few overnight affairs – most men seem to need them, don't they? – but that didn't matter. This time. . . ."

She broke off. Chin Ho, putting a match to his pipe, watched her blandly across the bowl, but made no comment.

Dorothy Harrington turned to him, said with a sudden vehemence, "I wish to God Milton had never taken on the refinery here. He should have sold out. He had a well-paid job as a chemist in California, and I wish like hell we could have stayed there."

Chin Ho moved his shoulders resignedly, lifted those expressive eyebrows in a rueful smile. "A lot of people think Hawaii is a paradise. But others can't wait to get out of it, I guess."

"I'm bored, Mr. Kelly. Bored. I think sometimes I'm going a little crazy. I need a man to lean on, Mr. Kelly, a man to talk to, to listen to me. . . . Maybe that's why I'm talking so dam' much now. . . ."

Chin Ho noticed that her hand was shaking as she took a long drag on her cigarette. A woman quickly developing into a neurotic, he decided, or even an alcoholic. Some drug-taking could easily follow: the old familiar pattern. The age-old story of the executive's wife who sees less and less of her husband.

Partly to change the subject, Chin Ho asked:

"Have you ever fired any servants?"

She shook her head. "On the contrary, we've always tended to over-indulge our domestics. They aren't all that thick on the ground these days."

"No."

After a moment he asked point-blank, "Did you ever hear of anybody called Mindoro? – Pedro Mindoro?"

She shook her head again.

"No, I'm afraid not, Mr. Kelly. But he may have worked for my husband, of course. I know nothing about the business side of his life."

"No, of course."

"Do you know my husband?" she enquired.

"No."

"He is a tall man – quite handsome."

"I've seen a picture of him in the *Advertiser*."

She looked out towards the sea again, a wistful expression slightly softening the cold blue hardness of her eyes.

"I was quite pretty myself once. But now I'm just a hag, aren't I?"

"That's nonsense," Chin Ho said.

"Milt is tired of me, I know that. When a woman gets to my time of life, her husband is easy prey to some sexy young whore, don't you think?"

She turned to look at him directly, and there was the hint of moisture in her eyes. He hadn't expected that. Mrs. Harrington didn't look the sort of woman who could cry easily.

"But if he wants a divorce, I'm not playing. I'm not giving him up, Mr. Kelly – never. I shall fight." Her voice was steady now, too steady, as if she were keeping it under too tight a control. He watched her drain the remainder of the highball with a quick backward toss of her hand.

Chin Ho swallowed uneasily. In her loneliness, she was using him as a conversational target, turning her thoughts into words and letting them tumble out. But this was all part of the job, getting close to human tragedy, getting to know the players in the drama. . . .

"I'm hoping that one day Milton will start to take some notice of me again."

"I think maybe he will," Chin Ho said. He knocked out his pipe against the chair leg. "I have to go now, Mrs. Harrington. I expect my office is beginning to wonder what's happened to me."

There was a strange look in her eyes as she said, "One day, Mr. Kelly, I may tell you something ... but not now."

He looked at her. "If it's anything of real importance...."

"No, Mr. Kelly, not now ... please. Perhaps later on. I'm not sure, you see ... not sure how things will go...."

She extended a hand. "*Aloha oe.*"

"*Aloha oe,*" responded the Five-O man, eyeing her curiously.

He was feeling slight pangs of sympathy for her as he left. But he was also puzzled.

What was it her conscience had told her she ought to reveal to him?

Why had she bitten back the words she wanted to tell him – for possible revelation at a later date?

Chin Ho was still thoughtful as he gunned the squad car and headed back along the old Farrington Highway towards Honolulu's City Centre and the Iolani Palace, home of Five-O.

CHAPTER SIX

The Iolani Palace – in which the Five-O team operated – formed a perfect travel-brochure building in the shimmering blue-and-white warmth of Honolulu.

The old palace of the nineteenth century Hawaiian monarchy – a monarchy now as extinct as some of Hawaii's numerous volcanoes – looked an incongruous and nostalgic oddity amid the towering concrete monoliths of the modern skyscraper-crammed city.

But if the tall palm-fringed building was reminiscent of a Mediterranean prince's palace or gambling-casino, there was nothing so frivolous about the determined men who worked day and night behind its walls in an endless struggle to keep the invaders from hell out of this earthly paradise.

Steve McGarrett looked at the temperature on the large thermometer hanging on the wall behind his desk, murmured "Phew," took a draft of pineapple-juice from the beaker just handed to him by his girl-Friday, Jenny, and removed his necktie – his only concession to sartorial laxity.

He looked across at Ben Kokua.

"What did you finally manage to dig out on Pedro Mindoro, Ben?"

Ben said, "Quite a bit, Steve. That's just a name he's adopted. His real name is Pedro Santos."

"Born in the Phillipines or here?"

"Neither, Steve. He's not even a Filipino. He comes originally from Cuba."

Steve stared at him and whistled softly. "Cuba? Holy cow, that accounts for quite a lot, doesn't it?"

"Yeah. Spawned by the Castro Revolution. A thoroughly

indoctrinated Marxist-Leninist. Illegitimate son of a dock-labourer, reared in slum hovel, never went to school, but as cunning as they make them when it comes to working for the elimination of the Boss Class and making himself a fast buck at the same time. All from CIA and FBI sources. Good job they don't burn their old dossiers."

"What else?"

"He moved around the Southern States of America for a period, trying to whip up a Black Power group. The FBI thought he was mixed up in illegal arms smuggling, but couldn't prove anything."

"And still can't?"

"They lost sight of him. It seems they were making things uncomfortable for him on the mainland. That's why we've got the bastard now, Steve – under a different name."

Steve got up and stood for a moment in the cooler atmosphere surrounding the electric-fan.

"I don't like the arms-smuggling bit, Ben. He could still have his contacts. Just switched his area of operations."

"It figures."

"The Union man said he was working for White Cross Mercantile, the shipping outfit and import distributors. I don't much care for the sound of that either, Ben. I guess we should put a regular tail on this guy for a bit. You look after that, Ben."

"Sure."

Steve looked out between the slats of the window's venetian blinds.

"Who are his friends? Has he got a girl, Ben?"

"Yeah. His steady girlfriend is half-Jap, half-Korean. Now and again they shack up together. Her name's Miki Shibata."

"And what does she do?"

Ben looked down at his notes.

"She helps the Superintendent at the Paradise Garden of Rest and Remembrance. That's a private burial-ground on the east coast near Makapuu."

"Anything known about her?"

"Not a lot, Steve. She's said to be intelligent, bit of a blue-stocking. Also a sporting and athletic type." Ben grinned and added: "Sounds like the member of a communist Olympics Team."

Steve did a little more pondering. Then: "Dig out some more about this brainy amazon, Ben."

"Okay, Steve."

CHAPTER SEVEN

The tall picket-fence thickly overgrown with purple bougainvillea made a useful screen for the Lincoln sedan that had purred quietly into position with Ben Kokua at the wheel.

The unobtrusive sedan – with not a single symbol on its shiny dark brown face to reveal that its driver was a Five-O man – had followed the old green Buick station-wagon all the way out to Makapuu, the first landfall of Oahu Island to be sighted by visitors arriving by ship from the mainland.

Here was a lovely landscape – a view straight through the magnificent *palis* of the Koolau Mountains, fluted brown and green walls of breathtaking splendour. The Paradise Garden of Rest and Remembrance was a beautiful place in which to enjoy your last long sleep.

The old station-wagon had seen its best days and was badly in need of a wash, but it had power enough, and Ben had been obliged to put his foot down now and again to keep the vehicle in view.

He felt pretty certain that Pedro Santos – alias Mindoro – at the wheel of the green station-wagon had been unaware of the normal-looking car keeping a tail on him.

All the same, Ben had not followed his quarry through the tall, ornate wrought-iron gates of the Paradise Garden, but had driven a little farther on, and had found a smaller secondary entrance to the cemetery grounds, one presumably used by maintenance and delivery men. Some way along this driveway he had found the useful bougainvillea-draped picket-fence.

From here he could see the single-storey flat-roofed

block of white office and store buildings standing at the head of the main broad gravel drive. Out from the administrative block radiated, like the spokes of a semi-circular wheel, other gravel paths, the latter bordered by smooth baize-like green lawns and the clean white kerbs and showy headstones of the tidily arranged graves.

The old green Buick station-wagon was now stationary alongside a door at the end of the office-block. It was the door nearest to where Ben was watching, and seemed to lead into a store section.

It was not far – say about a couple of hundred yards – from Ben's vantage point, but Ben had reached for his handy-sized commando binoculars before stepping out of the car.

Now, through a gap between trailing tendrils of bougainvillea Ben had a pretty good close-up view of Pedro Santos as the latter opened up the rear of the station-wagon.

Santos was a brown-skinned lean man of medium height, slim and wiry. From his thin swarthy face, topped by black curly hair, dark eyes burned fiercely with that smouldering aggression of the typical dedicated anarchist.

Ben guessed that a lot of women would find him handsome in a brutish virile way.

As he watched the Cuban open up the rear of the station-wagon, a girl came out of the door nearest to the tail of the parked vehicle.

Ben swung his binoculars on her as she walked towards Santos.

He knew now that he was looking at Miki Shibata.

A stockily-constructed young woman wearing an orange sleeveless round-necked blouse tucked into dark blue slacks. Hair arranged in a formidable helmet-like coiffure, its severity matching the slightly arrogant harshness of her broad flattened face.

Ben couldn't hear what she was saying to Santos, but he

calculated that her voice would be tense and emphatic. She would not know what it meant to be really relaxed. Not for her the famous Hawaiian philosophy of *hoomanawanui* – let's-take-it-easy, sweet-doing-nothing.

They had said the girl shacked up periodically with this sexy-looking Cuban. Yet they neither kissed nor touched each other on meeting.

Miki Shabata looked inside the station-wagon and gestured towards the door in the building behind them.

The Cuban nodded. His sinewy body bent forward into the station-wagon's interior. He emerged holding the rope handle at one end of a wooden box, dragging the box into the open.

The Korean-Japanese girl moved forward and took the rope handle at the other end of the box. Together they lifted it out – it was clearly quite heavy – and carried it between them through the open door at the end of the straggling white building.

Ben focussed his binoculars on the box. It was rectangular, some four feet long by a foot wide and a foot deep, the lid hinged and clasped and padlocked.

He watched the pair go inside the building and reappear about a minute later. They lifted a second, almost identical box, from the station-wagon's interior and carried this into the end section of the administrative block.

Finally both of them came out and stood for a few minutes talking earnestly, their faces revealing scarcely any animation. Then the man suddenly shut the rear door of the Buick.

Ben was a little puzzled by what he saw. The two were said to be cohabiting for most of the time, but if the Cuban looked outwardly as if he might be a competent performer in bed, the scowling girl certainly showed no visible sign of appreciating his sexual prowess.

Maybe it was a friendship based on something other than

the purely erotic attraction between *kane* and *wahine*, Hawaiian man and woman. . . .?

Pedro Santos could at least have given Miki Shibata a brotherly peck on her cheek before climbing back behind the wheel of the station-wagon. But he didn't. He merely waved to her and received a perfunctory wave back as he settled in the driving-seat and started up the engine.

The girl stood there for a few moments watching the old green station-wagon disappearing down the wide gravel driveway, through the fancy wrought-iron gates and out on to the Route 72 highway hugging Oahu's windward eastern coast.

Ben watched too, and presently – with an inner feeling of satisfaction – saw the girl go back into the building by way of a door further along the front of the low white building.

This meant that the room at the end of the block, into which they had carried the boxes, was now probably not occupied by anyone. It was almost certainly a storeroom of sorts, Ben decided, the office section no doubt being located further down towards the building's main entrance.

The door through which they had passed had been closed but not locked. At least, no key had been turned from the outside. Which meant that he could probably just turn the handle and walk in. . . .

An inner small voice shouted, "Be careful!" Steve McGarrett had often warned him against going solo, playing a lone hand, in situations where the risk-element was an unknown quantity. . . .

At such times, of course, it is better to enjoy the comfort of a snub-nosed Detective Special, a Colt .38, pressing cold and hard against the armpit. . . .

But Ben didn't enjoy any such comfort. Not at the moment. And no radio-link with the Iolani Police either.

Officially he was off-duty, if Hawaii Five-O men can ever be said to be off-duty. . . .

Hell, there were times when you had to decide to take a chance. And this was one.

He was ready to bet that Miki Shibata was the only one on the premises right now. Minding the shop alone. After all, things were pretty quiet on the funeral front.

Okay, Benjamin pal. You want to take a good look at those boxes, huh? – *inside* those boxes if possible. You're as curious as all hell.

Okay. So go in, Ben. Take a look. It's a great chance. Not a soul about, except maybe the souls of the dear departed.

The memorial-stone a few feet away from him, topped by a large winged angel with head bowed reverently, said: "In Loving Memory of Daniel Konomura, Departed This Life December 5th 1972, Aged 74. Mourned By The Many Who Loved Him."

Ben murmured "Good old Daniel Konomura," and slipped with one easy gliding movement behind the headstone.

And now, he realised, it was not going to be difficult to work his way towards that administrative block, a few yards at a time, by hopping stealthily from one headstone to the next.

The stones stood in a geometrically staggered formation between himself and that storeroom at the end of the block. There was a lot to be said, he thought irreverently, for the useful cover afforded by the more ornate stone memorials. But being quite sensitive by nature he tried to avoid doing any damage to the neatly-tended graves themselves.

When he reached the headstone that was nearest to the door through which Santos and his friend Miki had carried the boxes, there was only a short sprint in the open left to negotiate, across the few yards of gravel between the neat lawn and the white building.

Satisfied that there was nobody to be seen in the immediate vicinity, Ben braced himself and made the final dash. His hand closed around the handle of the door, twisted it. . . .

The door opened. Hell, that was a real stroke of luck. She hadn't yet locked it.

He pulled the door shut quietly behind him, and stood with his back to it for a moment, taking stock of his surroundings. He was relieved to find that he was alone and had apparently entered the building undetected.

The room in which he found himself was, as he had surmised, a sort of storeroom. The floor was of cement, the walls of whitewashed brick.

There was a single window halfway up one of the walls and a shaft of sunlight streamed through it to pick up the swirling particles of cement dust.

In the wall opposite the window was another door, at present shut, which presumably led into the Paradise Garden's offices and other administrative rooms.

In one corner of the bare white room, which was devoid of any kind of furnishings, were some wooden boxes and some large plastic bags containing what appeared to be fertilisers and hormone weedkillers for the burial ground's extensive areas of grass.

Ben was able to identify among the wooden boxes the two which had been carried in by the girl Miki Shibata and the Cuban Santos.

He got down on one knee and studied one of the boxes more closely.

A typewritten label stuck carelessly to the lid said: "FUNERAL ORNAMENTS. The Superintendent, Paradise Garden of Rest and Remembrance, Makapuu."

Some faint outlines of other printing showed through the

top label. There was another label underneath. Ben freed one edge and carefully peeled the top label off. Lucky, he thought, that it had been stuck only along the edges and not all over.

The label underneath announced: "SACRAMENTO MACHINE TOOLS INC." The consignment had been addressed to: "UNIQUE ENGINEERING CO., Iwilei." Another label, partly stripped off, said: "Per White Cross Mercantile Inc."

Unique Engineering Co., indeed! So unique that the Honolulu industrial estate of Iwilei, not far from the Harbour, had probably never heard of such an outfit.

The other box carried similar labels. Ben took hold of a rope handle and lifted one box off the ground. Hell, he thought, that was quite heavy. Metal, of course. Steel.

What kind of machine tools did a cemetery use? Well spades.... Did they make their own coffins? Carve their own memorial stones? But there were no facilities here for that. Then....?

Ben looked at the padlock securing the fastener of the box. A pretty resistant-looking job. Try to break it open? Almost impossible without some implement. Raise one corner of the lid?

He realised he needed some sort of prising tool. It would mean going back to the car, fetching something from the tool-bag....

He was still down on one knee, one hand resting tentatively on one of the boxes, when the creaking sound reached his ears.

The creaking sound, he knew, had come from no more than a few yards behind him, and it had suddenly set his pulses tingling.

The sound made by the hinges when a door is slowly opened....

Hideously conscious that somebody else was there, Ben

turned his head with an almost painful slowness, uneasy thoughts jostling in his mind, sharpening his faculties.

Miki Shibata was standing in the doorway looking at him.

Her dark blobs of eyes were sullen, impassive, acutely attentive, and dangerous.

CHAPTER EIGHT

Suzi Hayashi asked, her small oval face tilted sideways prettily: "Have you been to a massage-parlour before?"

Chin Ho Kelly smiled his bland smile and answered, "No. But I know now what I've been missing."

Her soporific fingers moved with dedication over Chin Ho Kelly's ample midriff. But it was not fat, she decided; it was hard firm muscle.

She said after a moment, "You didn't really come here for a massage, did you?"

Chin Ho blinked at her. "How do you mean?"

"I know who you are, you see."

"You do?"

"Uh-huh. Your picture was in the *Advertiser* just recently when you talked that girl out of jumping from the roof of the Rainbow Heights Hotel."

"I didn't deserve that," he growled. "She jumped off another one afterwards."

"You in Hawaii Five-O."

"Correct. Chin Ho Kelly. Call me Chin."

"I'm Suzi."

"I know."

"I know why you're here. You want to find out if I know anything about my sister – or rather my half-sister, Miki Shibata."

"And do you?"

"Yes. And sometimes I wish I didn't. It worries me more and more."

Chin muttered: "It worries *us.*"

"Oahu is a happy place," she said. "Well . . . it's happier

than a lot of places. Why do people want to change things? – make things worse"

"You know of such people, Suzi?"

"Yes, I know."

"And you want to tell me about them?"

She hesitated briefly. Then:

"I don't really want to get my sister into trouble, Mr. Kelly."

"It's Chin, Suzi."

"Miki has just got in with a lot of bad people, Chin."

"Looks like she has."

"She's got a good brain, but she always reads too many of the wrong kind of books."

"Political?"

"Yes. She puts politics before people. That's wrong, isn't it?"

"It happens," Chin said with a brief sigh.

He suddenly recalled a traditional Hawaiian saying: MALUNA O NA AUPUNI A PAU O KE OLA O KE KANAKA. "Above All Nations Is Humanity."

Five-O's work is mostly in the cause of humanity.

Chin Ho asked quietly: "You want to tell me about some of the things your sister is doing?"

"Not here," Suzi Hayashi replied, even more softly.

"At your apartment, then?"

She shook her head.

"I think I'm being watched, Chin. I think it's been going on for some time."

"Where, then?"

"At the Temple would be best."

"The Temple?"

"The Buddhist temple in Kalama Place – off of King Street. I go there regularly to worship."

"You do?" – his voice was surprised.

"I pray for peace and the end of violence. I pray that my

sister and her terrible friends will find a new love for their country. It is part of the Shinto belief."

She touched a responsive chord in the deep-rooted Orientalism of Chin Ho.

He said, "Confucius too preached loyalty to the State, the maintenance of law and order."

"I could meet you at the Temple later, Chin. Between four and five, say?"

"It's quiet there?"

"Yes, it is almost always empty. More is the pity. But there are too many Niseis. . . . Japanese people who have lost all contact with Japan."

"It's a date, then Suzi. I shall meet you there, and we'll talk." She nodded, her small face serious.

"If I should be delayed, wait for me," Chin added.

"Okay, Chin." She touched one of his feet. "And don't forget to wear your socks."

"Socks?"

"The floor is very cold. You have to take your shoes off before you go in."

"Ah, yes."

He was looking forward to talking to her again.

CHAPTER NINE

Miki Shibata stretched out a hand behind her and pulled the door closed. Ben found that small action comforting.

It meant that she was not going to scream for help, to call somebody from elsewhere in the building. And if she was not doing that, it was a practical certainty that there was nobody else there, that she was quite alone.

The orange sleeveless blouse was tight, concealing nothing but her flattish underdeveloped breasts. There was no gun-shaped bulge showing in the thigh pockets of her indigo-blue slacks. The bulge there was certainly no more than a handkerchief.

A woman on her own. Unarmed. He could cope with that.

Ben straightened up and smiled at her, an artificial display of cordiality which he felt sure would never work.

Miki stared back at him, face frozen and set in the hard mould of malice, the lips sensual and yet soullessly cruel.

The girl moved to the centre of the bare white room, placing herself between Ben and the entrance which he had used, watching him like a cat.

Ben smiled again, but less easily.

"I suppose I owe you something of an explanation," he ventured.

She shook her head and lowered it slightly, like a horned animal on the defensive. The shaft of sunlight from the window high in the wall picked up the highlights of the tight helmet of blue-black hair.

Then he realised that she was slightly crouching forward, her powerful hips and thighs and sturdy buttocks and hard small breasts straining against the thin material of her clothes.

She inched her way towards him, strong arms and hands probing at the dusty void between them.

Ben was suddenly conscious of the film of perspiration which had beaded on his forehead and upperlip.

Now she was poised in front of him, like an animal ready to leap, her amber arms moving like antennae.

Her face looked ugly, and Ben was faintly revolted by the odour of sweat rising up from the fuzz of dark hair in her armpits.

Feeling vaguely stupid, he found himself backing away from her. A sudden thought had come rushing into his mind to fan the small spark of fear.

She was half Japanese, half Korean. The Korean form of judo was perhaps the most deadly of all. Even though he was heavier by weight than the girl, it would make no difference.

Ben had taken some judo lessons once, but he had never progressed to Black Belt status. He had remained always the Kyu, the Pupil, never the Dan, the Master. A few exercises in the side breakfalls, roll breakfalls, the elementary throws (fifteen, was it?). . . .

Jesus, that was too long ago, too long. . . . The hairs on the back of his neck were crawling.

Miki Shibata was staring at him, taunting, challenging, maniacal. He was half afraid to move, because that first simple move would be an opening gambit and she would attack – mercilessly and with an exact and terrible science straight out of the academy of pain. . . .

Suddenly she pulled a handkerchief from her slacks pocket and hurled it at his face. And as Ben suffered a moment's obscurity of vision, the girl sprang at him.

It all happened in a few seconds, and he had no time for any kind of evasive action.

He felt the sole of her foot flat against his stomach, and her fingers tightly gripped the lapels of his jacket. Then she went down on her haunches and rolled backwards on to her shoulder-blades.

The foot on his stomach levered him upwards, and he was hurled across her head with incredible violence.

Ben crashed with a shattering force against a wall of the room, and for a few nightmare moments everything ceased to exist.

He became aware that he was on all fours, gulping in great choking lungfuls of air. A million flashing lights were advancing and receding on shock-waves of pain.

Ben clawed feebly at the wall to drag himself to his feet. Becoming half upright, he lurched forward towards her, drunkenly, stumblingly. . . .

And she was waiting, ready. . . .

First his arm was twisted unnaturally into a murderous nerve-destroying lock from which he could not escape without breaking his arm or blacking out from the agonising pressure on the nerve-point.

Then her hard sturdy buttocks were thrust against his crotch, her body half twisted, and the inevitable over-the-shoulder throw followed, propelling him for a second time like a stone shot from a catapult.

Remembering a little of his "breakfalls" instruction, Ben managed to strike the hard floor with the palms of his hands and his forearms, bending his arms in the act of falling, tucking in his chin to help protect his neck.

All the same, his head and shoulder thudded against the wooden boxes which she and the man Santos had brought in.

Once again there was a terrible roaring in his ears, ten times louder than the great Pacific breakers bursting on the Hawaiian beaches. The throbbing beats in his head were almost unendurable as the waves of agony and nausea pulsed through his being.

Christ, he thought, she would just go on playing with him like a cat with a mouse. Just throwing him against the wall until he was smashed, reduced to the boneless helplessness of a rag doll. . . .

Ben knew he couldn't let that happen. He must bide his time, play it cool. . . .

He lay there motionless for a while, leaning on one elbow, not looking at the girl but at a long cut on the back of his hand from which the blood had begun to seep.

Miki Shibata was standing over him, waiting for him to get up again. His nose picked up the musky odour of her woman-sweat. From the corner of his eye he could see, mistily, the violet-blue of her slacks.

He could not match her at judo, he knew that. She had probably gone beyond Black Belt . . . to the rare Red Belt even. . . . Had any woman achieved that?

Ben braced himself.

When his head became a little clearer, his vision slightly more in focus, he acted.

Pivoting his body in a wide scything motion, he crashed his legs sideways against the girl's.

She was totally unprepared for this sudden and quite unexpected tripping technique, even though it was not unusual in judo.

Momentarily she lost her balance. And those few seconds when she was caught off guard were all that Ben needed.

Not to perform any judo tricks, though. She was too high up in the Dan class for him to try that. This steel-framed little bitch would have graduated with full honours – in judo, karate, aikido, the lot . . . even maybe in "tae kwan do," the karate for killing used by the Korean troops . . . at least the "ate-waza," that blow on the nerve-ending that incapacitated . . . or that trick that ruptured the liver. . . .

Jesus, she had centuries of the artistry of pain behind her....

So no tricks, Benjamin.

No holds, no throws....

Just sock the goddam bitch....

A beautiful well-timed, well-placed haymaker worthy of Cassius Clay....

Ben was hardly aware of the violent movement of his arm forward and upward. He was hardly aware of the impact of his fist on her face.

He just knew that his fist had collided very hard with an obstacle, and that obstacle was the face of a girl.

It had not been a pretty face, and he had now made it less pretty.

It was the first time in his life he had struck a woman with his fist, and the realisation made him feel a little sick in his stomach.

He watched her crumple, and looked down at her prone figure on the dusty cement.

To hell with her and all her goddam kind.

There was a searing, stabbing pain reaching from his spine all the way down one leg. But his whole body felt bruised and aching.

He limped to the door that led out on to the gravel drive and flung it open.

Outside, in the harshly bright sunshine, he wiped the smarting perspiration out of his eyes. He screwed up his face and hurried, limping and hobbling, towards the place where he had left the car, every step an ordeal, the ground beneath him feeling insubstantial.

Every so often he glanced back over his shoulder, half expecting a bullet to come winging in his direction. He would make an easy target, and there would be no time to play hide-and-seek behind the tombstones, even if his battered body would allow such manoeuvres.

But luckily for Ben there was nobody to pursue him, nobody to fire at him. Their security was a bloody disgrace. But, then, the dead hardly needed protecting, did they?

Behind the picket-screen at last, he climbed painfully into the car, silently blessing the engine that spurted instantly into life.

Shutting the car door, releasing the handbrake, pushing forward the gear-lever, brought further spasms of pain to limbs that felt pulverised.

The Lincoln made its way out on to the highway, and sped off in the direction of Honolulu's centre and the Iolani Palace.

At the first traffic-light stop, he glanced down at a newspaper lying on the seat beside him. A bath-perfume advertisement said, "Parisienne – The Strong Favourite of the Weaker Sex."

The Weaker Sex. He began to laugh. And winced.

He remembered the joke about the cowboy with a redskin's arrow through his stomach. "Does it hurt?" – "Only when I laugh."

Ben laughed again. Winced again. In a job like Five-O it often helped to laugh.

CHAPTER TEN

Joseph Vladicek, who sat working quietly in the Paradise Garden office, had heard the Five-O squad car arrive.

It would have been impossible *not* to hear the arrival of an unusually angry and belligerent Steve McGarrett.

He had driven furiously all the way out to the south-eastern tip of Oahu, roared disrespectfully up the quiet, sedate drive of the Paradise Garden – which was more accustomed to decorous hearse-speeds – and stopped with a loud crunch of gravel and screech of brakes outside the main entrance of the office block.

The door of the squad car had been slammed explosively, and Steve had marched resolutely into the long white building and presented himself before the Superintendent in a manner that came perilously close to being downright militant.

The newest and most vulnerable member of the Five-O team – the likeable Ben Kokua – had been subjected to an unspeakable indignity, and Steve wanted to know what goddam right this two-bit Jap-Korean broad thought she had to perpetrate that kind of outrage on one of his men.

Steve had not gone to the burial-ground alone as Ben had unwisely chosen to do. He had his indomitable Number Two, Danny Williams, beside him to lend whatever support might be needed.

Joseph Vladicek was typing at an old Remington machine, picking out the letters with an unpractised slowness, when Steve came storming into his office with Danny close on his heels.

The man who had told Milton Harrington that he was Hungarian – but who might well have been a Soviet citizen

– raised the flat, unemotional Slav face under its unruly shock of thick blond hair and found himself confronted by the stern, buttoned-up face of the chief of Five-O.

"My name is Vladicek. Can I help you, sir?" – he was being deliberately – almost provokingly – imperturbable.

Steve said bellicosely, "You have a woman called Miki Shibata working here, and I want to talk to her."

The tall, broad-shouldered man rose unhurriedly.

"May I know what business you have with her?"

"You may, friend," Steve said brusquely, and whipped out his police identification. "McGarrett – Five-O. Miss Shibata, please – and fast!"

"Miss Shibata is not here," Vladicek told him with a carefully controlled patience coming close to insolence.

"She wouldn't be," Danny put in acidly.

"Check if she's here, Danno," Steve said pugnaciously. "I want that crazy goddam cow and I want her badly!"

Danny thrust his way unceremoniously into the room next door.

"I tell you she is not here," Vladicek insisted, his rather thin voice querulous. "But what are you claiming she has done, please?"

Steve glared at him.

"You know dam' well what she's done, Vladicek. Don't try pulling that innocent stuff, friend. I'm not having Five-O chased up a palm tree by any Red Monkeys. You get that, Tovarich?"

The big blond man with the pale poker face moistened his lips slowly.

"I think, McGarrett, that the boot is on the other foot, if I may say so," he said, picking his words carefully and with an exaggeratedly offended air.

"Meaning?"

"I mean that my young lady assistant was the victim of a

most vicious assault, carried out – I presume – by a member of your department."

"Jesus," Steve muttered, staring at him, "is that how you see it, pal?"

"What is Hawaii becoming?" Vladicek asked. "A police state?"

"With your help, comrade, it could become just that," Steve said. "And when that happens you'll never stop looking over your shoulder. Is that how you want it, Vladicek?"

The Slav was still unruffled.

"For all Miss Shibata knew," he said, "your man could have been burgling the premises."

"What do you steal in this place – corpses?" Steve countered.

"He had no right to be here, Mr. McGarrett. No right at all to enter this building without my permission. And, then – the last straw – to attack Miss Shibata like that!"

Steve stared at him disbelievingly. How did guys manage to twist their brains like this?

"You're joking, comrade? You've just got to be joking!"

"He struck her most savagely in the face, sir. Is this how your policemen enjoy themselves – striking defenceless women? Her face is very badly bruised and swollen. He might even have damaged her teeth."

"That's great," Steve said, smiling a malevolent, uncivil smile.

"She will probably lodge a complaint with the authorities," Vladicek added righteously.

"You tell her to do just that," Steve said grimly.

Danny came back into the front office, and slowly shook his head.

"She's not here, Steve."

"I told you she was not here," Vladicek put in petulantly. "As you might expect, she asked for the rest of the day off. She was extremely upset."

"You're breaking my heart, brother," Steve said ungraciously. "Could you tell us maybe where she went?"

"I've no idea where she went," answered the big blond man unhelpfully. "If you want to talk to her you must find her."

"Oh, we'll find her, friend. Of that you can be very sure."

Vladicek went on, "If you have no more business to attend to here, Mr. McGarrett, perhaps you would be good enough to leave. I have quite a lot more typing to do."

"Typing . . . yes."

Steve, as a sudden thought occurred to him, looked down at the Remington machine which had seen better days.

Vladicek had been typing out what appeared to be somebody's account for a burial. It looked innocent enough, Steve thought. But the type itself was much more interesting.

An uneven type of a kind which he had been looking at only recently. A rather worn ribbon, too. And the copying paper behind the carbon. A pale green.

The words of that original message came drifting back into Steve's mind as he looked at the paper in the machine. . . .

"The Officers of the Angry Battalion will meet at the usual place on Monday. . . ."

This was just an innocent invoice. But it could be quite vital as evidence.

Steve reached over and ripped the paper out of the machine. Vladicek reacted sharply, a hint of colour appearing in his cheeks, and the first faint glimmer of apprehension showing in his cold grey eyes – but only briefly.

"Now, look here, Mr. McGarrett. . . . !"

Steve watched the big blond Slav ball his fist momentarily, waited alertly, then saw the fist unclenched again as the man thought it better to get a firm hold on himself.

Vladicek watched sullenly as Steve folded the paper and put it away in a pocket of his jacket.

"You're really going a little too far, you know," Vladicek said, in a peevishly irritable tone of self-righteousness that the Five-O visitors found almost pathetic.

"And we're going even farther, comrade," Steve replied tautly.

"Meaning?"

"We're going through this building with a fine tooth-comb. How do you like that?"

"With what authority, please?"

"With the authority of the law of this nation, Vladicek," Steve answered inflexibly. "A just nation and a just law – which is something you and your kind find unacceptable. You'd like to change it all – is that right, friend?"

"I'm afraid I haven't the faintest idea what you're talking about," Vladicek said, shrugging wearily, shaking his large blond head in a show of bewilderment.

If he was worried, Steve thought, he was making a commendable job of concealing it.

Steve said bluntly, "Would you tell me what you have in those wooden boxes that my colleague saw carried into your storeroom today?"

Vladicek's brow creased in a puzzled frown.

"Boxes? We have quite a lot of boxes in our storeroom, Mr. McGarrett. Boxes that contain flower holders . . . metal rails for graves . . . that kind of thing. . . ."

"And what else?" – Steve stared him out. Not that this stony Slav was ever likely to come out the loser in a staring match.

"And, of course, bags and sacks of various kinds," Vladicek went on tolerantly. "We need fertilisers for the grass, for example. And sodium chlorate for the gravel paths."

"Sodium chlorate," Steve repeated. "Now, I find that very interesting."

Vladicek held his gaze unblinkingly.

"Yes, it keeps down the weeds, you know. Only on the gravel paths, of course. One needs hormone weed-killers for the grass."

"You don't say? And do you buy in large quantities of sodium chlorate?"

The Superintendent hesitated only the fraction of a second.

"Oh, no. Only enough for our immediate needs. It doesn't keep very well, you know. You are interested in gardens, Mr. McGarrett?"

"Just one, Vladicek. The Paradise Garden."

"Perhaps you would like one of our brochures?"

"I don't think your brochure would tell me the full story," Steve answered, continuing the staring match. "It wouldn't tell me what you kept in your store-room. Shall we take a look in there?"

Joseph Vladicek shrugged his shoulders and spread his hands. His face wore an expression of weary resignation.

"I've no idea what all this is about, but you may look in there with pleasure, Mr. McGarrett. The door is not locked. Please go straight through and study whatever you wish. I have nothing whatever to hide, as you will very soon discover."

Steve asked abruptly, "Have you ever heard of a man called Pedro Santos?"

Vladicek took a little time to ponder, then shook his head.

"Pedro Mindoro, then?"

The Slav's brow creased again, and he nodded his head slowly.

"Ah, yes. He is a friend of Miss Miki Shibata. He has

called on her from time to time. He is not in any trouble with the police, I hope?"

"Not *here* – as yet."

Vladicek went on, almost piously: "This is a respectable business we have here, Mr. McGarrett, as anyone will tell you. I would not want anyone here – either an employee or any friend of an employee – to get into trouble with the police. It would bring the place into disrepute. I wouldn't want that."

"I'm sure you wouldn't," Steve said ironically.

"I know that some people think we are just racketeers – charging prices that take advantage of the bereaved, they say – but our operations are completely above-board, Mr. McGarrett. Have there been some accusations made against me?"

"Christ!" Danny said incredulously. "I don't believe this guy's real!"

"Come," Vladicek said calmly, with an offended look at Danny Williams. "Let us go and take a look at the storeroom. I've really forgotten what boxes we have in there at the moment, but you're quite at liberty to examine the contents if that's how you wish to waste your time."

Steve McGarrett glanced sideways at Danny Williams. The latter was shaking his head hopelessly.

They both knew before they even looked that the particular boxes in which they were interested would no longer be there.

CHAPTER ELEVEN

The temple in Kalama Place was empty, and strangely cold considering the clinging warmth of the Honolulu air outside.

Suzi Hayashi found the silence and the emptiness vaguely disturbing, although she had not been affected this way before.

The temple was like a small lonely island, cut off from the hustle and bustle of Honolulu's busy streets only a matter of yards away.

She knew that the spirits of the dead were here in the temple, and their influence floated all about her.

There were tiny black tablets here, the *ihai*, like miniature gravestones, one of which bore her mother's name. She would sometimes sit on the floor, and place the tablet in front of her, and pray to the spirit of her dead mother for guidance and help. The Tablets of the Dead could be a comfort. They would never comfort her half-sister Miki, unless Miki could be saved.

This afternoon she left the tablet where it was, near the feet of Buddha, and knelt before the bland-faced effigy of the great Gautama.

The ample proportions of the fat, placid, calmly smiling idol only served to accentuate the smallness and butterfly-lightness, and the frown of distress, of the girl who worshipped in silence and the shadow of fear.

Suzi Hayashi, kneeling with bowed head, closed her eyes and buried her small oval face in her upturned palms. Her lips moved in soft whispered utterances.

Faintly in the distance she could hear the thin screaming of a jet-plane coming across the Aloha Tower to land at the

Honolulu International Airport, but it seemed to belong to a quite different world – not to this silent shrine, where the whisper became a roar, and the pungent smell of incense-tinder smouldered slowly in a fat gilded vase.

The gods – the spirits of the dead – seemed to be whispering back to her, and the whispering seemed to echo, a low humming sound, in the deserted temple.

"You are about to die, Suzi Hayashi. Soon, very soon, you will be with *us* . . . the Lotus Gods. You will say Sayonara to the wickedness of the world, the evil of your sister's friends. Your own sins of impurity have offended us, but we shall forgive you, our sister, and take you into our keeping. . . ."

She shivered slightly and wished that Milton Harrington were at her side to comfort her. But Chin Ho Kelly, the kind man from Five-O, would do . . . anyone would do. . . .

Her ears picked up the sound of a quiet movement behind her . . . right behind her . . . the soft padding sound of feet . . . the rustle of a sleeve . . . right behind her. . . .

She wanted to turn her head, to look up, but she was afraid to move, and remained as still as a statue in a niche. . . .

The big strong arm descended suddenly, swiftly. It wound itself fiercely, mercilessly, about her neck, pinning her head so that she could not move it an inch. . . .

The arm pressed hard against her slender throat, forcing her head backwards, so that she stared with protruding eyes, at the temple's red and gold ceiling. . . .

She wanted to cry out, but only a choking, gurgling sound, like the death-rattle itself, bubbled up out of the small rosebud mouth . . .

CHAPTER TWELVE

Steve McGarrett was in one of his most dynamically aggressive moods, which meant that before many more *leis* had been hung around the rubber necks of Hawaiian tourists some heads were going to roll under the implacable Five-O axe.

His rugged face wore the skin a bit tighter than usual. The muscles at his jaw-hinges were working overtime. And every so often Steve would thump fist into palm to drive home a point.

Watching him, Ben Kokua felt his self-confidence slowly creeping back. He was feeling somewhat better than when he had first arrived back at the Iolani Palace, but, all the same, the effects of being catapulted twice against hard slabs of brick and cement were going to take more than a few hours to wear off.

"One thing's come out of this, Steve," Ben said, attempting to put a good face on the situation, "we know pretty certainly now how Eddie Hastings died. Those heavy bruises . . . that broken neck . . . they were never the result of Eddie falling off a horse and rolling down a short escarpment into some boulders."

Steve looked up as his secretary Jenny came into the room, and murmured "Thanks" as she handed him a tall tumbler of pineapple-juice.

"Eddie had been cultivating Miki Shibata for some time," Danny interpolated thoughtfully, "knowing only too well that she was among the top brass of the Angry Battalion. Eddie was probably all ready to spring the whole story – as he had told the Governor he would at that Labour Day reception at the Sheridan-Waikiki – and he might even have hinted as much to Miki Shibata."

"And that would justify Eddie Hastings being sentenced to death by this mob," Ben elaborated. "It's rather unusual for a girl to be appointed executioner, but the set-up in this case was just dandy, Steve."

"Yeah," Danny put in, picking up the unstoppable train of thought. "She innocently suggests going riding with him up on Koko Head. That's to be the execution ground. And in that little nest of boulders where they found his battered body Miki Shibata kills him by means of judo. Remember that Eddie Hastings was a small, light man. That murderous bitch would toss him around like a can of beans."

"It figures, Steve," Ben said eagerly. "Who could never prove definitely that Eddie had *not*, in fact, bruised his body and broken his neck in the fall from his horse and the tumble down that slope into those stones?"

"Sure, it figures," Steve agreed, rubbing his chin. "But if nobody could pin anything on the Shibata dame *then*, how the heck do you do it now? These hoodlums have got it all nicely sewn up."

Danny said, "According to the report of the inquest, she claimed that she rode home first and left Eddie riding on his own. Maybe we could dig up something to prove she *didn't ride home until after* the time of Eddie's death?"

Steve got to his feet and paced up and down a little between his desk and the window.

Then he stopped, facing them.

"No, Danno. Don't let's waste time on that right now. It's not likely to stick, anyway. This other aspect is much more important. The threat to State security. Agreed?"

"Agreed, Steve," Danny said.

McGarrett was looking towards Ben, who was trying to hoist himself from his chair and finding the effort a strain on his injured back.

Steve said seriously, "Ben, I want you to get X-rayed pronto round at Queen's Hospital. Okay?"

"It's nothing, Steve," Ben said, suppressing a wince. "I'll be okay."

"Do you want to start a fight with me, Ben?"

"No, Steve."

"So you go and get yourself a clearance from Queen's. Okay?"

"Okay."

Danny grinned, but the grin died quickly as the telephone rang on McGarrett's desk – that peculiar twitter which Hawaiian telephones have, creating a sound midway between the chirping of a cricket and the cooing of a pigeon.

Steve grabbed the receiver.

"Five-O. McGarrett."

The voice at the other end was unmistakable. The voice of Chin Ho Kelly, crisp and businesslike, and yet palpably tinged with sadness.

Steve listened, his expression becoming steadily grimmer, as Chin Ho presented his report over the wire. He nodded as he listened, scribbling an occasional note on his desk-pad.

Finally he replaced the receiver slowly, and, after a brief moment of meditative silence, looked across at Danny and Ben.

"That was Chin ringing in," Steve announced soberly. "He went to see Suzi Hayashi, Miki Shibata's half-sister, at the Lomilômi massage-parlour on Maunakea Street – that's where the kid works. She told Chin she had something on her sister Miki."

"That could be a real lead," Danny broke in with enthusiasm.

"No . . . no help, Danno. The kid promised to talk to Chin at the Buddhist Temple in Kalama Place, off King Street, because it's quiet there. The kid seemed a bit scared. So Chin went there. But he was too late."

"She'd gone?" Ben asked.

"Gone to Nirvana. She was dead."

"Holy cow," Danny murmured. "Murdered?"

"Looks that way."

"Silenced," Ben said.

"Chin's on his way back pronto with the full story," Steve went on. "Looks like things will start warming up from there."

Ben smiled, and said: "Don't try grounding me, Steve, when the action starts. Even if I had to go on crutches, I'd still want to be there when we put that muscle-woman on the rack."

Steve said, "Crutches? You been in some trouble, then?"

*

"The kid was garrotted," Chin Ho Kelly reported, not liking what he had to tell them.

"Strangled from behind?" Steve prompted.

Chin Ho nodded. His face looked genuinely sorrowful.

"Did the HPD boys find anything?"

"Footprints," Chin Ho said.

Steve shook his head disappointedly.

"It's a temple, Chin. People would be in and out. Footprints everywhere, I guess. How the heck do you sort them out?"

"Easy, Steve," Chin Ho answered, and half-smiled at his chief. "Only *one* person's footprints there."

Steve gave him a sharp, quizzical look.

"One?"

"Nobody ever enters the place without first removing his shoes. It's a must, Steve. Suzi thought it important enough to mention it to me."

"And the killer didn't?"

"That's right. Evidently not a worshipper. And the impressions of the killer's shoe-soles led in a straight line to where they found the girl – and then led straight out again. Just the one trail of shoe prints, Steve – in and out. Kind of eerie."

"And a lucky break, Chin. What were they like?"

"You'll be hearing from Che Fong presently."

"Great. The HPD photographer took pictures?"

"Uh-huh. Che was given prints as soon as they were ready, Steve. I guess the Lab will come up with something we can use."

"Stir them up, Chin. I want it fast."

*

Steve bent studiously over the photo-print lying on his desk.

It was an enlarged picture of the sole of a shoe.

"That's the clearest one, Steve," Che Fong told him.

Che Fong, the Chinese-Hawaiian who had become the principal forensic scientist in the Five-O Laboratory which was buried away in the lower regions of the Iolani Palace, had laid the blown-up print on Steve's blotter.

"What do you make of it, Che?"

The brilliant laboratory man answered, "Well, I'd bet my last dollar it's a woman's shoe."

"Pretty large," Steve remarked.

"Yeah, on the large side for a woman's. A heavily-built female, I'd say. But the shape looks more like the shape of a woman's shoe."

Steve took a magnifying-glass from a desk drawer and held it against the picture.

"There's a distinct kind of pattern on the sole."

"Yeah," Che said. "A bit broken up, but we'll do a drawing of what the complete pattern looks like. The pattern is rather unusual, I'd say. Shouldn't be too difficult to trace it back to one particular shop."

"We could do with that information. Work on it, Che."

"Okay, Steve."

Che Fong left the office and hurried back to the Five-O Lab.

Steve said firmly to Danny Williams, "We shall need some evidence that will stand up in court. But, meanwhile, I'm going to work on the theory that Miki Shibata is our woman."

"And if we can't get her for the Eddie Hastings killing," Danny responded with an air of satisfaction, "we might get her for her sister's homicide."

"And one *attempted*!" Ben put in ruefully, looking up from some rather tedious paperwork to which Steve McGarrett had assigned him.

"Yeah – right!" Steve said, adding his own half-grin to the much more extrovert one on the face of the more ebullient Danny Williams.

Ben was looking a trifle unhappy. Like all the Hawaii Five-O team he greatly preferred action to sedentary desk work.

The Queen's Hospital radiographer had not taken long to pronounce Ben Kokua "sound in wind and limb," but "probably ought to take things quietly for a day or two."

Ben had not been born to take things quietly. He impatiently awaited that well-known one-word command from Steve – "Go!" – when swift action was the order of the day.

Steve slapped the desk suddenly.

"Danno, I'm going to put out a general call through Central Dispatch! I'm going to have that homicidal amazon picked up before she provides any more customers for that graveyard guy she works for! Lay it on, Danno!" He jerked his head towards the office radio-transmitter.

"Okay, Steve!"

"And they'll want a description of her." Steve glanced towards Ben.

"Ben will just love to give a full description of Miki Shibata. That right, Ben? But watch the language, brudda, huh?"

CHAPTER THIRTEEN

"Look, don't tell me I'm nagging again, but it's time you went back downstairs, Miki. It's not safe you being upstairs. Suppose they turned up all of a sudden . . . a kind of raid?"

The Cuban, Pedro Santos, spoke with a worried earnestness. His lean brown face, under its shock of untidy black curls, wore a harassed expression. The small muddy-brown eyes had a hunted look in them.

The Korean-Japanese girl regarded him broodingly.

"Stop yakking, Pedro, for Christ's sake," she said in a hard, irritable voice.

Santos averted his eyes. He knew that she didn't like him staring at her damaged face. Part of her jaw was still badly swollen, and of a yellowish-purple colour.

From Ben Kokua – without love.

Santos stood staring out of the window. A Venetian blind had been dropped over it so that nobody could see in. The blind-slats were slanted to provide a view across and below.

The room, rather sparsely and poorly furnished with old second-hand furniture, was quite large and on the ground floor of one of the nineteenth-century houses which had managed to survive the onslaught of the Aloha State's busy bulldozers.

The house was in one of the old streets west – or *ewa*, as the Hawaiians say – of Ala Moana Park. It lay close to famed Fisherman's Wharf, alive with local colour, where the tripper-boats sailed for Pearl Harbour, and a tuna-fish-cannery, shacks selling antique bric-a-brac, sampan-building workshops, and old tenements with sagging balconies made crazy but picturesque bedfellows.

"They're out looking for you, you know that," Santos said, combing his thick black hair with thin nervously restless fingers.

"And suppose they find me?" Miki challenged.

Santos swallowed painfully.

"That newspaper guy . . . Hastings . . . Jesus, they might still get on to something. . . ."

"Let them try."

"Then that joker from Five-O . . . and . . . and. . . ."

She glared balefully at him. "He assaulted me, didn't he? Look at my face. I could say the son-of-a-bitch tried to rape me. Who's to say he didn't?"

Santos shrugged his shoulders, made thinner-looking by the tight-fitting, soiled T-shirt stuck with sweat to the bony brown body.

There were some newspapers and books lying on the seat of an old bamboo armchair. Miki Shibata picked a book up and idly thumbed through the pages.

"I could do with a bath," she said peevishly. "I'm stinking like an old River Street whore."

"It's too risky," Santos snapped out crossly. "They could turn up here any minute. They know you spend some time at this place – you can bet your life on that. It's where they'll come looking."

"It's terrible downstairs in that goddam cellar," Miki said. "It's hot down there. Airless. Like a goddam dungeon. I have to come upstairs sometimes just for a change of air."

"Oh, sure, sure," Santos agreed, "but don't stay up here too long, that's all. It gets me all on edge."

She threw the book down on the chair in a gesture of annoyance.

"You've done nothing but bellyache just lately," she said spitefully. "Jesus, you make me want to throw up sometimes."

"God-dammit," he said in an aggrieved tone, "I didn't ask you to hole up here. It was your own idea."

"There was no place else to go," she flung back at him. "Anyway, you do all right out of the Movement. They pay you for the use of that room downstairs. Okay?"

Santos buttoned his lips tightly. He went on staring out between the blind-slats, straight down to the far end of the street, past the motley collection of ancient and new buildings.

"You were always a yellow-belly," she taunted him in her brittle, soulless voice. "You're so goddam yellow, there are times when you get positively neurotic."

Santos didn't deign to answer. He just kept his thin back very straight, his shoulders pulled back. Her words came at him with the force of blows. He didn't think he could stand much more. Maybe he'd go back to Havana, back to his own kith and kin. Or maybe he'd start taking drugs again. . . .

Miki went on vindictively, "Remember when you got high on the 'weeds'? You did it for your nerves, you said. And what did it do for you? – just tell me that – what did it do for you?"

"Uh, forget it, willya?" he said. "Just forget it, for God's sake."

"You made a bomb out of sugar and S.C. You jumped the gun, right. You set it off outside Henry Mackeson's house. If that wasn't a dam' crazy thing to do."

"The bastard asked for it."

"Our Leader could have killed you for that. You know that, don't you? He doesn't want anybody starting trouble all on their own. That's just begging Security to come and sniff us out, right? The Leader wants us to work together when he gives the signal . . . when it's right for the Big Day. Okay?"

"Okay. Okay. I said forget it."

"But what about the job at Harrington's place? Did you get high on the 'weeds' again, Little Man?"

He brought his fist down on the back of the bamboo chair.

"Christ Almighty, I've told you I never did that! I've told you a hundred times!"

"But maybe you were so high you didn't even know what you were doing?"

"Oh, Mother of God! Just believe me, baby, I didn't do that! Just believe me for once, huh?"

She shrugged her muscular shoulders – a shrug that managed to combine contempt and incredulity – and picked up the book again to browse through it sulkingly.

But presently she was droning on again. Her voice had not the pretty musical quality of her sister, Suzi Hayashi. It was a monotonous, aggravating, low-pitched hum.

"Just remember," Miki said, "The Leader will decide the moment to strike – when and where it will hurt most. We're still preparing . . . planning. We have to wait a little longer. We must both try to keep our heads . . . to be patient."

She was trying to convince herself, not him, Santos thought. She could see failure staring them in the face, but refused to admit it.

There had been the unwelcome attention from the journalist-pig. He'd got what was coming to him, but how much had he passed on?

Then that Harrington-pig had got on to Miki's sister. Miki had watched them meeting at that temple. Why had they met there? Harrington had been chummy with the newspaperman, hadn't he?

Then that Five-O-pig had come poking and prying around the Paradise Garden place, and *he'd* nearly gone to his Maker too.

Jesus, it didn't look good. It made you shiver. But he

owed it to the rest to stick. . . .

Santos said suddenly, "Christ!"

She saw his back stiffen, not from wounded pride this time but from a sudden stabbing of fear.

Miki laid the book down on the chair and said, "What? What's the matter?"

"There's a police car at the other end of the street!"

She snorted venomously, "Let the pigs come!"

Santos rounded on her wildly.

"Don't be a stupid bitch!" he shouted at her, bordering now on hysteria. "Get back downstairs. There's no time for goddam arguments!"

"How do you know they're coming here?"

"But they *may* be!"

"Okay, Little Man," Miki said levelly, her lip curling. "I'll go down there. But you're real scared, aren't you? Jesus, you're so scared, you could wet your pants."

Santos, ignoring her, was already at work, the sweat beginning to bead freely on his low forehead.

The room in the spacious old nineteenth-century house – split up into separate apartments – was fairly long and lofty.

At one end of it was a big Dutch-colonial-style dresser constructed of yellow pine, but for some time now it had not carried on its shelves anything in the way of china or glass. This dresser carried nothing but cheap brassware, some calabashes, and bowls made from the wood of the Hawaiian *koa* and monkeypod trees.

Nothing fragile or breakable on *this* dresser. That kind of decorative feature would never do on a dresser which had to be moved every so often.

The perspiring Santos was now feverishly pulling it away from the wall against which it stood. The effort made the veins brand his forehead.

When the base of the old dresser was moved, and the

carpet below it lifted, it was seen that there was a hinged trap-door cut out of the wooden floor.

Santos raised the trap-door hurriedly.

"Hurry up, for God's sake hurry up," he hissed at her.

"All right, all right," she answered moodily. And, with a reluctant obedience, she stepped through the opening in the floor and on to the long flight of wooden stairs leading down into what had once been a wine-cellar.

Her movements were unhurried and carefully deliberate. Santos wondered if she ever got excited about anything – really worked up.

Maybe another woman could stir up some passion inside her . . . some emotional warmth? A man could arouse a little, but never the maximum. Her hermaphrodite instincts often disgusted him – and yet, strangely, they could be attractive as well as repulsive.

After a moment she switched on the light in the cellar-room. It was quite clean and dry down there and furnished with a long table and several chairs. A ventilator high in one wall and an electric-fan kept the temperature reasonably tolerable.

This was where the officers of the Angry Battalion held their periodic meetings.

"Okay, I'm going to close the door again," Santos called down to her.

The trap door was lowered, the threadbare carpet replaced, the big clumsy dresser pushed back into position against the wall.

By now Santos was shaking a little and struggling to gain control of himself. He wiped the sweat from his brow with his forearm.

He stood near the window, but not too close to it. After a moment his breathing was more in check and the slight twitching in his face had stopped. The tightness of his mouth was loosening, and the hands, trailing by his side, became more relaxed.

The outline of the police-car was now clearly visible, quite close. But there was no whirling red light, no banshee-screaming of sirens.

The car cruised slowly, quietly along the street. It slowed down with an exquisite sense of delayed torture, and stopped near the peeling old house whose ground floor and basement were used by the members of the Angry Battalion....

"When we have achieved our objectives, you will have shaped the way the world is marching," the Leader had said to him.

He must hold on... calmly.

The Cuban's stomach felt sickly empty, but he stood his ground and waited....

*

"Okay, Chin, you move around the back," Steve said to Chin Ho Kelly, now completely in command. "Danno, you stay with me."

The big heavy front door, which was kept unlocked, opened when Steve turned the handle. It was apparently the communal entrance to the house, the apartments being self-contained.

Another door facing them in the small lobby bore the figure "1" above a glass panel. A faded piece of cardboard just below the bell-push said in mauve ink:

"P. MINDORO."

"Okay," Steve said to Danny Williams, "this is the joint."

He prodded the bell-push.

After a short wait, the door was opened. Steve hadn't been certain it was going to be all that easy, and drew in a tiny sigh of relief as he glanced at Danny.

Santos, alias Mindoro, narrowed his eyes at his two visitors as if they had been unexpected. He was keeping a tight grip on himself, stifling the turbulent nausea inside him.

"Yes?" – the word was made to sound casual and dismissive.

"McGarrett – Five-O," Steve said and flashed his official card at him. "You can maybe help us, Mr. Santos."

"Mindoro," Santos corrected calmly.

"Santos," Steve contradicted.

"And so?" – the tone just hinting at truculence.

"You know a girl called Miki Shibata?"

The Cuban appeared to weigh the question up for a few moments. Then, with an attenuated smile: "She's a girl who sleeps with me now and again. Have you made any new laws just lately against screwing a dame?"

"No, Mr. Santos-Mindoro, but we do have a few regulations connected with murder and offences against the security of the State. Do you want me to lay it out for you?"

"You can lay out just whatever you like, copper," the Cuban said. "Just see where it gets you."

"You want to tell me something about your friend Miki Shabata?"

"Maybe I should call my lawyer?"

Steve's stare was of cold steel. "I've been a cop a long time, Santos, and I never met anyone who needs a lawyer more than you do."

There was a slight nervous movement in the Cuban's throat.

"Where is she, Santos. Is she holed up here?"

"Why do you think she has to be holed up at all, copper?"

"It's a long story, comrade. You just tell me if she's here. Or do we have to bust our way in and look for ourselves?"

Santos stood to one side, half bowing in a mock show of politeness.

"You don't have to bust your way into any place, Mr. Law-Man. You can just walk in quietly and look around." He made an expansively sweeping gesture with his arm. "Be my guest, huh?"

Steve exchanged a quick glance with Danny. Then, with his eyes still firmly fixed on Santos' face, he said, "Okay, Danno, let's take him up on that."

They walked past Santos into the big sparsely-furnished old room.

The Cuban leaned insolently against the big dresser and watched them make a circuit of the room, taking in every small detail as they went.

"The other rooms?" Steve snapped at him.

Santos answered with a curt nod: "Kitchen through there. Not very big, the kitchen. You can see the little patch of garden through the kitchen-door. . . . Oh, and don't forget the bedroom on the left." He smiled thinly again. "That's where the real work's done when I'm on the bed with Miki. Only she isn't on the bed right now."

Moving around the place briskly, Steve looked in all the rooms, under the bed, in the cupboards, while Danny remained by the side of the Cuban in the big living-room.

When the Five-O chief rejoined them, Santos enquired with a brief flash of bravado, "You gotta big case against me, copper?"

McGarrett replied, "We'll build one, son – as high as the Aloha Tower. But, as of now, we have enough on you to keep you on ice until we're ready to throw the book at you."

"Tell me all, McGarrett."

"I'll tell you enough, comrade. Using explosive to cause wilful damage to private property. Aiding and abetting and harbouring a murderess. Plotting to cause the breakdown of law and order. You want more, friend? – like suspected trafficking in illegal guns?"

Santos' face was now shiny with sweat, and the nervous tic had returned to one cheek, but he managed to produce another impudent smile.

"Guns, Mr. Policeman? You mean water-pistols maybe? Me working in the docks."

"You going to tell us where Miki Shibata is?" Steve flung at him.

Santos spread his hands. "How should I know? I'm not her keeper. Maybe she's shacked up with some other bum?"

Steve flexed his jaw muscles. "That's very helpful, comrade. I'll remember how beautifully you co-operated."

"Wait!" Danny Williams exclaimed suddenly. "Wait a bit, Steve. . . ."

"Yeah, Danno?"

"Look . . ." Danny said.

He pointed to the books and newspapers lying on the seat of the bamboo armchair.

Steve looked, and his eyes met Danny's as if by appointment.

"He's illiterate, Steve – remember?" Danny prompted.

McGarrett swivelled his gaze to the Cuban.

"You can't read, Santos. How come you've got these egghead books? – this week's newspapers?"

A look of alarm that he was unable to conceal flickered across the face of Santos.

"A friend left them here."

"A friend?" Steve echoed witheringly. "Would that friend be Miki Shibata?"

"And is she still here? – did you bring in these things for her to read, at her request?" Danny fired at him.

"Dammit, you looked everywhere, didn't you," Santos

challenged. "You had the run of the joint!" He sneered. "Maybe she managed to get herself inside that suitcase on top of the bedroom closet!"

As soon as he had said it, he quite clearly wished he hadn't.

"Suitcase," Steve said, snapping his fingers. "I never thought...."

He made a hurried dive towards the bedroom. Santos watched him go, his eyes a little wilder-looking and more afraid.

After a moment, Steve came storming back into the living-room. He threw a pair of female panties, a girdle, two pairs of women's shoes on the floor in front of the startled Cuban.

"Do you wear these, chummy?" he demanded sternly. "Maybe you're a *mahu*, huh?" In Hawaii a *mahu* is a man more interested in other men than in girls.

"Wait, Steve..." Danny put in quickly. "Those shoes.... You looked at the soles?"

"Yeah," Steve answered abruptly, "but they're not large enough, anyway."

"Then....?"

"Let's forget that for now, Danno," Steve said, his face a taut mask, eyes cold. "Let's just think about Miki Shibata ... about her being *here*...."

"Okay, Steve."

McGarrett turned his head to look out for a moment between the slats of the blind over the window. His eyes widened.

He swung back to face Danny.

"The old houses down here have cellars, Danno! You read me? Danno, we're slipping – we nearly forgot that, didn't we?"

Steve looked at the Cuban, and now the Five-O man's face was really iced over.

"Okay, Santos. Talk – and talk fast. How do you get down into the cellar?"

Santos gazed back at him. There was suffering in the Cuban's eyes, a suffering born of pent-up terror that screamed to erupt. His lips moved to say something, but his tongue seemed to be frozen in his mouth.

"Tell me where and how you get down there! If you don't, comrade, we'll give you such a goddam roasting that you'll finish up like a *kalua* pig at a *luau* feast!"

The Cuban's counter-stare was no match for the fierceness of McGarrett's.

Santos' mouth became slack. He swallowed. He jerked his head sideways, launching a shower of sweat at the same time.

"The dresser," he murmured in a half-whisper. His face was bleak with defeat. He knew that for him, at least, it was the end of the road.

Steve moved across the room quietly. He pulled the big dresser away from the wall. Then methodically he raised the carpet and lifted the trap-door.

Miki Shibata's voice called out from below, "Have they gone, Pedro?"

Steve called down the stairs, "Come up, Miss Shibata!"

Danny put in quickly, "Watch it, Steve! Remember what she did to Ben!"

"Good thinking, Danno."

Steve pulled the Colt .38 Special from his shoulder-holster.

"She doesn't carry a rod," Santos told him.

"She doesn't need one," Danny retorted wryly.

"Okay, sweetheart," Steve called down the stairs. "Come up slowly. We're waiting."

After a few moments Miki Shibata appeared, a sullen arrogance in her bearing.

Steve covered her with the revolver as she stepped from

the top of the cellar stairs on to the floor of the living-room.

The girl looked a little contemptuously at the gun and attempted a smile, but the smile belonged only to her mouth, not to her eyes. There was never any real humour in Miki Shibata's eyes.

"We're going to book you, baby," Steve said.

"On what charge?"

"As a beginning, let's try attempted homicide."

"You gotta make that stick."

"We'll use glue," Steve said.

The strain of the past few minutes had proved altogether too much for the Cuban. Something inside him snapped.

The thin brown man made a sudden wild lunge towards the door into the kitchen.

Steve and Danny heard him fling open the kitchen-door, heard the door crash against a wall. But they made no attempt to move.

The voice of Chin Ho Kelly was just audible to them in the big room.

Chin Ho was saying to Santos, "You aiming to go some place, buster?"

It really *was* the end of the trail for Pedro Santos, alias Mindoro.

CHAPTER FOURTEEN

Steve McGarrett looked from the window of the wedding-cake-structured Iolani Palace, out across the wide forecourt fringed by tall palm trees whose tousled heads were stirred gently by warm Hawaiian zephyrs.

A motley crowd of dark-spectacled tourists moved about down there to form ever-changing kaleidoscopic patterns, sporting hats made of coconut-leaves, wreathed by *leis* of sweet-scented flowers bought for a few dollars from the *lei*-stalls at Honolulu Airport, dressed in vividly-coloured *aloha*-shirts, and *muumuus* – those extraordinary garments seen everywhere in Hawaii, like loose-flowing, ankle-length nightgowns in dazzling flowery patterns.

Happy people, all bent on the harmless pursuit of pleasure, and there was plenty of happiness that day – and every day – on the beautiful island of Oahu, in spite of the darker aspects of the island's life which kept the Five-O men perpetually on their toes.

A group of people had, it seemed, dedicated themselves to destroying the well-ordered democratic system which had made such beauty and such innocent happiness possible.

They aimed to use violence to strike at an established society, the evolution of which began with good old King Kamahameha, whose giant statue out there, one hand firmly gripping a barbed spear, stood as a symbol of Hawaii's indestructible freedom.

The rigorous processes of long-established law – of which the Hawaii Five-O squad formed a vital part – would alone provide the antidote to the poison.

As the thought passed through Steve's mind, he saw a

smart Oldsmobile pull into one of the marked-out parking spaces only a few yards from the wide stone steps leading up to the pillared and balustraded balcony running across the front of the Iolani Palace.

The car looked different from the others. It had the "executive" look, a businessman's car, quietly impressive.

Steve watched intently as the driver locked the door of the car. There was something familiar about the car's owner, and Steve realised that he knew him, that he had seen him before and not too long ago.

He had, in fact, talked about him to Danny Williams the night they had been entertained out at Schofield Barracks, the same night that they had heard the bomb-blast and witnessed the leaping up of the flames from the bomb-wrecked private bungalow over on the westward side of the island.

He had recalled to Danny how they had met the man at a Union conference at the Waikiki Biltmore. And now Steve was able to remember the meeting in greater clarity.

He knew that the man leaving the status-symbol car and walking with a slight stoop towards the home of Five-O was the sugar-refinery man, Milton Harrington.

Steve had, in fact, been expecting him.

The Governor had rung the Five-O office a little earlier.

"I've been talking to Milton Harrington, Steve . . . the sugar chap. I know him quite well, of course. We meet from time to time at the Royal Hawaiian, as I think I mentioned before. . . ."

"Yes, Governor."

"It's been some little while since I saw him, but now I've met him again, and he's a changed man, Steve. I've never seen a guy look more downcast or more ill than Harrington looks right now. And it can't be just the result of that bomb scare out at his bungalow. . . ."

"I wouldn't think so, sir."

"No, Steve, it's my opinion that there's something much more serious on his mind.'

Steve said gropingly, "You mean things happening at his refinery? – things in connection with the matter we're investigating?"

"I don't know, Steve. He didn't go into detail. But when I hinted that Five-O had picked up some Leftie militants who might well be responsible for the damage to his property he reacted at once – pretty vehemently."

"You think he might be able to tell us something?"

"Yes, Steve, and it was very obvious to me that he *wanted* to talk. So I told him to talk directly to you. He'll be on his way over, I guess. It could prove very interesting."

"I agree, Governor."

"Let me know what happens. I quite like Harrington. And I don't relish seeing a fellow deteriorate mentally and physically."

"I'll let you know, sir."

The Governor kept his finger very firmly on the pulse of Hawaii. Few things ever escaped his attention or failed to hold his interest.

And now Milton Harrington was here, looking a rather incongruous figure in his dark grey worsted among those swarming tourist throngs who emulated the picturesque dress of the natives.

Presently Steve's secretary, Jenny, came in to announce that Milton Harrington was actually in the outer office.

"Okay, Jenny, show him in."

Steve pulled out a drawer of his desk, flicked a switch. Harrington would not be aware of it, but the ensuing conversation would be recorded on tape.

When Harrington came through the door, to be greeted with a friendly handshake by the Five-O chief, Steve was as surprised as the Governor had been at first sight of the refinery man.

On the occasion of that earlier conversation with Harrington at the Waikiki Biltmore Hotel, the middle-aged businessman had looked much fuller in the face, more healthy-complexioned, younger in his general posture.

But now, Steve noted at once, his visitor had a grey, drawn, almost haggard appearance, with tell-tale semicircles of dark beneath his eyes. His shoulders seemed to droop as he sat down, at Steve's invitation, in the chair on the other side of the desk.

For his opening gambit, Steve said, "I understand you met the Governor at the Royal Hawaiian and that he told you of some of the progress we're making against the island's political hotheads. . . ."

"Yes, Mr. McGarrett, but I wonder if your progress is fast enough, or if you are dealing with these people rigorously enough."

Steve raised his eyebrows but decided to say nothing, preferring to let his visitor do most of the talking.

"I daresay you remember Eddie Hastings of the *Advertiser*?" Harrington went on, his face creased by the sudden pain of the memory.

Steve nodded.

"Eddie was a great friend of mine, you know. We got on very well together. I was terribly shocked by his death, Mr. McGarrett."

Five-O's chief executive nodded again.

"But no matter what the autopsy said, I don't believe for one moment that Eddie's death was accidental."

"Nor do we, Mr. Harrington."

"You mean you think he was murdered?"

"We feel pretty certain he was, but it's something that we might never be able to prove. We can possibly book the guilty people for other crimes."

"I'd like to be able to pinpoint the bastards who killed Eddie," Harrington said emotionally.

"I think you can safely leave that to us," Steve answered.

A little of the tension disappeared from Harrington's face, as if experiencing a feeling of relief.

"I'm very glad to hear you say that, Mr. McGarrett. It's one of the reasons I came to see you."

"Just one of the reasons?"

Harrington briefly hesitated, then continued, "You know about the Angry Battalion, I suppose?"

The question came as a slight shock to Steve. The subject was classified Secret, and the name had been kept pretty closely under wraps.

Looking at his caller fixedly, and glad now that he had remembered to set the tape-recorder working, Steve asked: "And how do you come to know about the Angry Battalion, Mr. Harrington?"

"Through a message typed on a sheet of green paper," replied the man on the other side of the desk. "I sent that piece of paper anonymously to the Honolulu Police Department."

"So it was you," Steve murmured.

"I realise now that it should really have come direct to Five-O since your department is more concerned with matters of State security."

"Correct. But let me understand this right, Mr. Harrington. Why did you think it necessary to conceal your identity in this matter? Did you imagine you would be implicated in this plot to subvert the Constitution? Were you afraid of these people?"

Milton Harrington shook his head slowly. He paused to offer a cigarette to Steve but the Five-O man declined. Steve watched him light the cigarette with a hand that was shaking slightly.

"It wasn't fear. I was afraid of being implicated, yes, but not as a political extremist . . . a traitor." He looked at the tip of his cigarette. "I was having an affair, you see, with the girl who gave me that typed message from the Angry Battalion."

Steve nodded.

"You mean Miki Shibata's sister?"

"So you've at least got that far?"

"Oh, yes."

"Her half-sister actually. Suzi Hayashi."

"Yes, we know that too."

"I thought that if the police began asking questions about where I'd got the Angry Battalion message, it was bound to come out that Suzi Hayashi was my mistress. I suppose I should have had more courage."

"We are all human, Mr. Harrington."

There was a brief period of silence while Harrington, sitting very still, watched the smoke curl up slowly from his cigarette.

Then the refinery man looked up at his host, and Steve observed, with some surprise, that tears had begun to form in his eyes.

"The thought of that girl dying so violently has been more than I can stand, Mr. McGarrett. . . ."

Steve made no reply.

"Suzi Hayashi was a sweet, gentle girl – not at all like her sister," Harrington said with deep feeling. "She was the sweetest girl I ever knew, Mr. McGarrett. Her nature was so warm and loving that she would never have hurt a fly."

Harrington was fighting hard to control the emotion which had brought tears to his eyes.

He went on: "She was bitterly opposed to the people her sister had got mixed up with. She wanted to keep the Hawaiian way of life exactly as it is."

"We know that too, Mr. Harrington," Steve informed him. "She intended to co-operate with us."

Harrington continued: "For a long time she was torn between loyalty to the State and loyalty to her sister. The latter was clearly quite mistaken."

Steve nodded again.

"I was in love with her, Mr. McGarrett, more deeply in love than I'd ever been before. And I would readily have married her if only I'd been free. Does that shock you?"

"On a racial basis, do you mean? Naturally not. The different races freely intermarry in Hawaii."

"Yes, that's true," Harrington admitted. He sat slightly hunched drawing tobacco into his lungs. "What I meant was ... I was not sure what your personal feelings were about the ... the sanctity of marriage."

Steve answered thoughtfully, "I guess that depends on the kind of marriage you have."

"That's right. And mine is a prison," Harrington revealed, staring hard at the Five-O chief. "Can you imagine marriage as a kind of fortress-prison, Mr. McGarrett? – a sort of Colditz? – with its own stone walls and iron bars?"

"I guess it might look like that to some, Mr. Harrington."

The sugar-refinery man was drawing extra heavily on his cigarette. He regarded Steve McGarrett with slitted eyes through the blue haze of smoke.

"When you're deeply in love with a wonderful girl like Suzi, and you feel that you've got to get out of that goddamned marriage-prison at any cost, Mr. McGarrett ... well, you get crazy ideas. . . ."

Steve studied the face on the other side of the desk. He guessed at the manic-depressive psychosis which had set in following the murder of his close friend and then, even worse, the murder of his mistress.

"How crazy, Mr. Harrington?"

"You think it might be a good idea to blow that prison up – or rather, maybe, to blow up the cold god-damned cow of a woman who represents the barrier to your real happiness. Do you follow me, Mr. McGarrett?"

There had been no mistaking the repugnance in Milton Harrington's voice as he poured calumny on his wife Dorothy.

"Are you trying to tell me, Mr. Harrington, that you saw the Angry Battalion movement as a good alibi for murder?"

Steve was icy calm as he watched Harrington stub out the cigarette-end in the ashtray with a slightly trembling hand.

"Are you saying that you yourself planted the bomb that wrecked your wife's bedroom that night?"

Harrington said, "I do know how to make them, you know. I was a chemist."

"You actually planted that bomb?"

"Yes. I bungled the job badly, didn't I? The bitch had gone out by the time it went off. But I put it there okay."

Steve bit hard on his back teeth.

"You realise that you've just confessed to attempted murder? – that I've got to book you?"

Milton Harrington shrugged his shoulders resignedly. His face looked smudged with fatigue, and it was clear that he cared no longer about anything.

"There is just one other thing," Harrington added, almost as an afterthought.

"Yeah?"

"Suzi had one last throw. . . ."

He took out his wallet, extracted a folded sheet of pale green flimsy paper, and tossed it on to the blotter on McGarrett's desk.

"She gave me that the very last time I saw her. It's another Angry Battalion message. I guess she stole it from her sister's handbag. That's how she got the other one. She took a hell of a risk. . . ."

"Yeah, sure."

"You'll see it mentions a date a few days from now . . . a date when the anarchists expect to put their initial plan into action. . . ."

Steve's face stiffened. His eyes flickered to his visitor.

"This is very useful, Mr. Harrington, and I'm grateful to you. Being helpful in this way should do something towards making things easier for you."

Harrington attempted to smile, but it was painfully forlorn and weary.

"You know, Mr. McGarrett, there's a bit of Eddie Hastings in you. I like you. It's a pity we can't see more of each other."

"Maybe we will, Mr. Harrington," Steve said. "Maybe we will."

Almost reluctantly he reached for the telephone to get the HPD escort for the sad, tired man facing him.

CHAPTER FIFTEEN

Steve McGarrett, with his jacket off and his necktie loosened, had one hand resting on the desk telephone as if anticipating it to deliver another of its Aloha purrs.

Both he and Danny had spent an exceptionally busy hour on the telephone, both making and taking calls. The indefatigable all-purpose Jenny of the outer office had not been idle either.

It was one of those days when everybody – but everybody – was jumping like a Mexican bean.

Under Steve's other hand, gripping a ballpoint, was a notepad. On the pad was a series of "Action" tasks. Most of them had been ticked off as having been performed. It always surprised everyone that a man who could be so useful with a Colt .38 in tight corners could also be such a methodical desk-man.

"Holy cow," Steve murmured, pausing a moment to sip at the tumbler of pineapple-juice dutifully placed on his desk by Jenny, "let's hope these sugar-barons don't give us a loud horse-laugh and think we're just a bunch of scarey nuts."

Danny Williams growled, "Hell, those sugar-daddies would come down on Five-O like a ton of their own large cubes if they ran into some kind of trouble that we hadn't warned them about."

"That's the story of our life, Danno," Steve retorted. "We can't win 'em all."

"I think we've just about covered the lot, haven't we, Steve?"

"Yeah. Jenny will double-check."

All the sugar companies had been systematically forewarned to:

Double their security arrangements during the next few days, especially during night hours;

Maintain a close watch on any employees suspected of having extreme left-wing views;

Instruct all gatekeepers and security-officers to examine any suspicious boxes or packages introduced into the refineries: the latter could contain sufficient sodium-chlorate to form a dangerous mixture if introduced into sugar crystals in the centrifugal drums, or granulators, and subsequently ignited by time-controlled detonators or incendiaries;

Reinforce fire precautions and train senior staff to deal with any emergency or panic arising from the anarchists, disruptive measures if any of these should prove successful.

At the same time HPD men were detailed to keep a close watch on island industries – such as dyeing – in which sodium chlorate was sometimes used, and all companies selling sodium chlorate for weedkilling purposes.

Nothing was to be left to chance. It was always better in Five-O's view to be over-cautious than not cautious enough.

Sugar had been the most important thing in Hawaiian life for more than a century.

It was sugar which had led to another revolution towards the close of the last century. A stormy night of unrest and fear. The eventual seizure of the Treasury. The intervention of US Marines. The taking of Hawaii under American protection. The imprisonment in a room of the Iolani Palace – the very headquarters of Five-O – of the then Hawaiian Queen ... that Queen who composed the haunting "Aloha Oe", "Farewell to You"....

Things had moved fast, on that occasion, between revolutionaries and counter-revolutionaries. Hawaii had not been such a happy, smiling place then.

Nothing like that must ever happen again.

It was Five-O's job to kill such an insurrection in the

bud stage – with special briefings to the chiefs of the Honolulu Police Department and the Commanding Officers of the local defence forces.

Five-O itself stood ready. Ready for anything.

The next important thing for the Five-O men to do was to make certain sure that they got to any concealed arsenal before the insurgents got there.

In this connection, the sudden return of Ben Kokua to the office – he had been out on some special leg-work with Chin Ho Kelly – brought the real highlight of a tense and slightly frenetic day.

Ben was looking specially elated. He was evidently ready to live up to his name – *Kokua* – which in Hawaiian means "to help."

He had obviously forgotten – at least temporarily – those severe bruises and abrasions which had only very recently made him wince each time he turned his handsome head or sat on his *okole* or Hawaiian backside.

"Steve!" he proclaimed excitedly to his chief. "I've got it! I've got it!"

McGarrett raised a quizzical eyebrow.

"I know where they're storing their armaments!"

Steve looked at him with the bright eyes of a man enjoying every minute of his job.

"Spill it, Ben."

"That Paradise Garden burial-ground, Steve . . . some of the people there are really dead . . . but some aren't!"

Danny and Chin Ho broke into a smile despite the underlying sobriety of the theme.

"When I was in the Paradise Garden that day, Steve, I noted the name on one of the headstones . . . a guy called Daniel Konomura . . . and the date of death. I checked out with the registry of deaths."

"And the death wasn't registered?"

"Oh, sure! They played it really legitimate, Steve, all

along the line. But the *address* given for Daniel Konomura was phoney."

Steve raised his eyebrows.

"It didn't exist?"

"It *used* to exist, Steve. But it was bulldozed out of existence for a new development long before Daniel Konomura died."

Danny Williams whistled and said, "Interesting."

"That's what I thought," Ben continued exultantly. "I went straight back to the Paradise Garden and checked on a few other names in the vicinity of Konomura's grave – they're not easily visible there from the office and store block, so I was able to do so without being spotted."

"Good work, Ben," Steve said. "And?"

"I followed through those names too, and traced the addresses given at the time the deaths were registered. The story was the same every time, Steve – the places had been knocked down by property-developers a long time before the so-called 'deceased' actually died."

"Are you sure about this, Ben?"

"Positive, Steve."

Chin Ho put in, by way of an elaboration that was already a little behind McGarrett's leapfrogging mind:

"You see what that means, Steve. There were burial services with all the ceremonial trimmings for phoney dead people – Angry Battalion members playing the mourners, I guess. The coffin was duly lowered into the grave. Everything perfectly in order on the surface. Flowers and all, you bet."

"Beautiful," Steve murmured, a hint of admiration in his voice. "I like that. That's beautiful."

Ben added, "But was there any dear departed in that expensive satin-lined box? like hell there was!"

"Guns," Chin Ho interpolated with a tiny smile of glee on his broad oriental face. "That's where the Angry Battalion armament went, Steve – and where it could remain in perfect safety until they wanted to use it. There isn't any doubt that there *were* guns and ammunition in those boxes Ben saw Santos deliver there."

"Pedro Santos managed to get the guns brought in by way of White Cross Mercantile, the outfit he worked for," Ben rattled on with evident zeal. "They were ostensibly machine-tools shipped over from the mainland for a non-existent Honolulu engineering company. They were then intercepted by Santos, relabelled as 'funeral ornaments,' and the boxes delivered to the Paradise Garden by Santos himself in his station-wagon."

"To be interred as soon as possible as corpses – people who never died – and never lived," Chin Ho wound up. "You like the theory, Steve?"

"I like it a lot, Chin. It's real dandy. Good work, boys."

Steve leapt impulsively from his chair like a spring-loaded jack-in-the-box.

"Well, this is it, fellas," he said enthusiastically. "We're going to work on the assumption that this theory of yours is the right one. We're going to indulge in a little desecration. Let's hope the island gods won't object, Ben. . . . Okay?"

He took the shoulder-holster containing his Colt .38 Special from the bottom drawer of the desk and strapped it on in a businesslike way.

"Better we all go suitably equipped this time. . . . Danno? – Chin? – Ben? Okay?"

They nodded and set about equipping themselves with their police-issue revolvers.

"Right," Steve said, a hard glint in his eye, "let's get this office on the road, huh?"

CHAPTER SIXTEEN

The Five-O squad car, with a lot of power in its entrails, didn't exactly dawdle on its twenty-minute-or-so drive out to Kakapuu, on the island's eastern tip.

Danny Williams was at the wheel and enjoying that away-from-the-office freedom which affects policemen as well as the people who perform mundane jobs.

Beside Danny sat Steve McGarrett, poker-faced and impassive, but happy with the way things had gone so far.

In the rear of the roomy squad car were Chin Ho Kelly and Ben Kokua, both with closer Hawaiian ties than the American *haoles* (pure whites) in front of them, yet no less impressed by the unceasing miracles of the Hawaiian landscape, dominated by those fluted and cloud-capped Koolau Hills.

It was hard to reconcile their mission with the peaceful scene.

Down on Makapuu Beach, the sun-lovers would be leaping in the transparent turquoise sea or lying stretched out on honey-gold sands under feathery palms. Along there at Whaler's Cove, the educated dolphins would be performing their feats for the tourists. At nearby Kaneoke Bay the tourists would be gazing at the under-sea coral formations through glass-bottomed boats.

All so beautiful. So relaxed. A great big garden of paradise.

But the keen men in the police-car thought principally of the Paradise Garden of Rest and Remembrance, the place to be buried in style, the place where you found eternal peace. . . .

Peace among the rifles and small arms. . . .

Arms from America to create chaos in America's Fiftieth State. . . .

Fidel Castro's coup in Cuba could never have happened without those ruthless assaults by Castro's young men – armed with sporting rifles smuggled from America. . . .

As they reached the section of the highway on which was located the main entrance to the Paradise Garden, Ben touched Danny on the shoulder.

"Start slowing down a bit, Danno. The entrance with the big wrought-iron gates is a couple of hundred yards ahead. . . ."

"But I go past that?"

"Right. For another couple of hundred yards. There's a secondary driveway – narrower – the 'tradesman's entrance,' you might say."

"Okay."

The squad car made the approach carefully, turning slowly and quietly into the driveway.

"A little way ahead there's a vine-covered screen," Ben told him. "I guess it's where they dump the unsightly things that would spoil the ritzy appearance of this gold-plated Boot Hill."

"Okay, Ben, I see. . . ."

"I parked behind that. It makes good cover."

"Yeah."

Danny killed the engine quietly.

Steve said in a low voice, "We don't know if anyone is in earshot, so don't slam the car-doors. Okay?"

Steve got out, pushed the door to with a soft click.

His eyes swept the immediate vicinity.

"Okay, so far. . . ."

"Wait!" Chin Ho said in a loud whisper.

"Chin?"

"I can see a couple of guys, Steve. I guess you can't see

them from where you're standing. The headstones block the view from some angles. . . ."

"Let's look. . . ."

McGarrett stood up close to Chin Ho.

"Yeah. One of them is Vladicek. They're carrying a wooden box too."

Danny joined them.

He said, "We didn't meet the other guy – the one with the Zapata moustache."

The Five-O men caught periodic glimpses of Joseph Vladicek and his companion as they made their way towards the office-and-storeroom block. They would disappear and reappear, second by second, as they passed behind the serried rows of gravestones, some quite ostentatiously large.

Ben said, "That's the same kind of box that I saw before."

Chin Ho, standing in a slightly different place, said, "From here, Steve, I can see where they've been working."

"They've opened a grave, Chin?"

"Yeah, I can see the mounds of earth . . . freshly dug."

Steve said, "Great. That clinches it, I guess. The hunch is paying off."

Ben, itching to go now, asked, "Do we rush 'em?"

Steve said sharply, "No, we wait. They've got a car on the gravel over by the storeroom. If we rush 'em now, they'll have time to jump into the car and beat it."

"We let them get inside the storeroom?" Danny prompted.

"Uh-huh. Then when they're inside, we rush 'em. Okay?"

They nodded their understanding.

"Wait, though," Steve said thoughtfully. "We don't know how many they've got there. Danno, radio Dispatch, to send their nearest patrol-car. If we lose out, they'll take over."

Danny said, "Lose out? Us?"

"They've got arms in there, Danno. They could use them."

"Sure."

"And Danno. . . ."

"Steve?"

"Bring the loud-hailer. We might have to talk to those creeps long-distance."

"Sure."

Using the stone memorials for cover, the Five-O men moved forward a few yards, and presently, Danny, his radio message transmitted, joined them at the double.

Progressing towards their goal in a series of quick, darting sprints, keeping out of sight as much as possible, they made their way through the ranks of stone crosses, marble scrolls, obelisks, solemn angels and chubby cherubs.

They had only a few yards more to go to reach the gravel drive that fronted the storeroom when a bullet whanged through the quiet air of the garden-necropolis.

The bullet – a heavy one – smacked into a headstone and flung tiny chips of stone and dust into Chin Ho's face.

"Oh, Momma Pele!" Chin Ho exclaimed, invoking a well-known Hawaiian goddess. He hurled the whole of his ample body behind the headstone.

The others were already taking cover behind the protective memorials.

"Hell and damnation!" Steve cursed. "They've spotted us!"

Ben slid his head an inch or two beyond the edge of the stone behind which he was taking cover.

A gun bellowed again, noisily. The bullet whined within millimetres of where Ben's head had been.

"This nut can shoot," Danny commented.

Ben said, "They've pushed open a window to the right of the door. That's where they're firing from."

Now Steve showed himself briefly. And as the expected shot ricochetted between the cherubs and angels, showering dust and fragments over the neat grass of the graves, Steve fired almost simultaneously in a quick reflex action, counterpointing the heavy bark of the anarchist's gun with the sharp businesslike crack of his own.

There was the noise of shattered glass, and Chin Ho grinned at Steve.

"That one will cost your Dad the price of a new window, Steve."

"Shall we take a chance and rush?" Danny called across.

"Too risky, Danno," Steve said. "That sounded like a Thompson SMG they've got there. They're using single shots, but they could spray us with a round of thirty as we ran across there. So we hold our horses, Danno."

"Sure."

Steve said, "Let's have the loud-hailer, Danno."

Danny tossed the loud-hailer across a gap between the headstones and Steve caught it. He brought the hailer up to his mouth.

"Drop your weapons, Vladicek, and come out with your hands on your heads!"

The sound of Steve's voice went rippling across the quiet and deserted cemetery.

There was no reaction from the storeroom. Steve spoke through the amplifier-horn again.

"Wise up, Vladicek! You haven't a chance! Nothing will happen to you if you come out with your hands up! You got that?"

There was a shout from the direction of the window.

Steve said, "What did he say?"

Ben smiled. "It sounded like 'get screwed,' Steve."

Steve shouted again through the hailer.

"Police reinforcements are on their way! You will be outnumbered badly, Vladicek! You haven't a cat-in-hell's chance! You understand me? So come out, Vladicek! Come out while you've got the chance!"

There was a lengthy silence. It was broken only by the distant wailing of a police-car siren, and the sound was coming nearer.

"Happy music," Chin Ho said cheerfully.

"Hey, look!" Ben yelled.

Their eyes followed the direction of Ben's finger.

Vladicek and the man with the Zapata moustache had suddenly emerged from the main office entrance at the other end of the block. They were carrying automatic weapons.

"Smart bastards, eh?" Steve muttered angrily.

He leapt a space between headstones to lie down behind a stone grave-kerb.

He laid his .38 Special on the kerb and got Vladicek in the sights.

The barrel spat flame.

"You got him in the shoulder, Steve!" Ben yelped happily.

Vladicek had been running towards the wrought-iron gates of the Paradise Garden's main entrance. He suddenly stopped, clutching his shoulder. There was a spreading bloodstain on the Slav's pale blue shirt.

And now Vladicek swung round to face them again, but still on the move, backing towards the gates.

There was a quick stuttering burst of automatic fire from the Thompson M1 he was carrying. Bullets spattered wildly among the gravestones. Chips of stone flung themselves stingingly on the back of Steve's neck as he lay against the side of the grave with his head well down.

Slowly he lifted his head. He levelled his .38 and let off another shot.

It missed Vladicek, but hit the man with the Zapata moustache. Steve saw the latter stumble and go down.

Vladicek was still running backwards, his face creased with pain. He released another burst with the sub-machine-gun.

Steve fired again, but as soon as the bullet had left the revolver he knew that this last shot had been unnecessary.

The HPD patrol-car, its siren screaming and roof-light flashing, roared through the gates into the Paradise Garden.

Vladicek never had a chance.

"Jesus," Danny murmured, peeping around the side of a stone that said "At Peace Forever."

There was an ear-splitting screech of brakes as the police-car driver almost thrust his foot through the floor.

But it was too late.

The car ploughed relentlessly into the fleeing Slav.

Vladicek had become an ugly mess of blood-drenched flesh and splintered bone.

He had found eternal rest in his own beautiful, classy Paradise Garden. But without ceremony. Without a satin-lined casket.

Steve yelled through the loud-hailer. "We're Five-O, fellas – don't shoot!"

And the Five-O men went running to greet the HPD men.

CHAPTER SEVENTEEN

"That's her over there, Steve," Chin Ho said, nodding his head, and Steve took a good look at the woman who walked alone in the Airport Gardens.

The Oriental and Polynesian Gardens around the terminal building at Honolulu International Airport are alive with the sight and scent of flowers. They vie with the blossoms being sold in the form of *leis* from stalls built like Hawaiian huts.

Piped music competes with the droning announcements over the public-address system of arrivals of the big Boeings from Los Angeles, Tokyo, Sydney, Hong Kong.

Tourists in their bright *aloha*-shirts, voluminous *muumuus*, kimonos, and what-have-you, add to the vibrant colours of the scene.

Dorothy Harrington was an incongruous figure in such a setting. She just didn't belong. She walked entirely alone, slowly, her face dead pan, staring at – and yet through – the noisy, rainbow-hued sights and scenes around her.

She looked lost, like a dead soul in limbo. Now and again she swayed a little, and passed a hand across her eyes.

Steve and Chin Ho fell into step alongside her, and Steve said, "Mrs. Harrington?"

She turned and looked at the Five-O chief with scarcely any expression in her eyes.

"Yes?"

Then she looked at Chin Ho, and said, "Ah, yes. . . . I know *you*, don't I? It's Mr. Kelly?"

"Yes, ma'am," Chin Ho said.

Steve showed her his card.

"I'm McGarrett – also from Five-O."

"Ah, yes." She said it as if she had been expecting them.

Steve looked at the Pan-Am holdall she was carrying.

"Going away, Mrs. Harrington?"

She said, "I have a sister in Los Angeles. She invited me to stay." She wavered a little, then added: "I never wanted to go back to our bungalow on the West Coast, you know – not after one side of it was almost completely wrecked. . . ."

Her speech was slightly slurred, and Steve occasionally detected the stale aroma of alcohol on her breath. He remembered that she drank rather a lot these days. Chin had mentioned that.

"As your Mr. Kelly knows, I've been staying in a private suite at the Makaha Inn, not far from our bungalow. . . ."

"Yes, I know," Steve said.

She was not an unattractive woman, he thought. Rather too big and heavy to be called graceful. But the large body had kept its shape. It was not too bad for forty.

At the moment her make-up looked rather botched, her eyes were looking pitifully tired, and her facial skin looked loose and weary.

Steve advised her gently, "I don't think it would be a very good idea for you to leave Honolulu right now."

She looked at him with strangely dead eyes.

"There's a Boeing 747 leaving in an hour, Mr. McGarrett, and I'm supposed to be on it."

"I wouldn't worry," Steve consoled her. "I'm sure Five-O will arrange for the refund of your flight money."

"Yes . . . I see." The face of the tall blonde was unemotional. Her expression was disconcertingly vague as if she were having some difficulty in marshalling her thoughts.

"As you know," Steve said, "we're having to hold your husband in custody pending his trial on a charge of attempted homicide. He's confessed, Mrs. Harrington."

"To trying to blow me up?" She nodded, her eyes taking on a hint of bitterness.

"It's rather bad for a wife's ego, Mr. McGarrett, when her husband wants to get rid of her so fast that he tries to blow her to hell."

"Yeah, I can understand that."

She added flatly, "I *knew* he was responsible all along."

Steve glanced at Chin Ho quickly and said, "You knew?"

"Yes. I knew when Mr. Kelly came to see me at the Makaha Inn. I ought to have told him then. But I went on hoping and hoping that relations between Milton and me might get back to what they used to be . . . when we first got married. . . . You know?"

"Sure."

"A servant of mine – Nani – a Hawaiian girl – saw him at the bungalow when he was not supposed to have been there . . . and behaving suspiciously. Nani was supposed to be away, too, but she had changed her mind. Milton thought she wasn't there . . . that the bungalow was empty. . . ."

"Yes, I see."

"After that bomb had gone off, I guessed what he had done, you see. Nani knew, but said nothing."

"I wish you'd told me, ma'am," Chin Ho said.

"Yes." She nodded dejectedly. "There was never any chance of Milton coming back to me, I suppose. . . Not while. . . ."

"While Suzi Hayashi was his mistress?"

Her eyes were pained. She looked away, stared into the distance at a plane circling before coming in to land.

After a moment, she said, "I knew they were meeting. I followed him."

"Yeah," Steve said.

"And that's the chief reason why you want to keep me here, isn't it, Mr. McGarrett?"

"You've been expecting it, I guess?"

"Yes."

Chin Ho told her, "We found shoe-prints in the temple, Mrs. Harrington."

She regarded him apathetically.

"Mine?"

"I've been out to the Makaha Inn. They showed me the shoes that you left there," Chin Ho continued. "The rather unusual pattern on the soles matched the shoe-prints in the temple. And I can tell you more, Mrs. Harrington. You bought them at a shop in the Hilton Hawaiian village. Right?"

"I didn't think you'd take very long to find out, Mr. Kelly. But I'm not sorry, you know."

"Not sorry that you strangled Suzi Hayashi?" Steve asked.

She shook her head. "No, not sorry things have come to a head at last. I think I *am* sorry I strangled Suzi Hayashi. It was an impulse thing. She looked a rather sweet little thing . . . like a butterfly.

Steve made no reply.

"You want me to go with you, Mr. McGarrett?"

"I should like that, Mrs. Harrington."

"Very well."

They walked together, like tourist strollers, into the terminal building, Steve on one side of her, Chin Ho on the other.

She said, "Funny isn't it. . . .? You get involved in a sordid domestic situation and it leads you into all sorts of other things."

"Other things?"

"The island is buzzing with rumours that Five-O have uncovered an anarchist plot to kidnap the Governor."

"I wouldn't believe everything you hear, Mrs. Harrington."

"There is just one thing I should like to do before I leave. . . ."

She nodded towards a pair of doors for "Wahines" and "Kanes."

"Ladies" and "Gentlemen."

She attempted a smile, humourless and bloodless.

"The Powder Room? Sure . . . we'll wait."

*

They got a United Air Lines stewardess – crisp, efficient, giving off friendliness as a stove gives off warmth – to look in the Ladies' Powder Room, because she happened to be passing at the time.

An American girl, oozing charm and yet combining an ability to remain completely unruffled. But stewardesses are supposed to be like that, aren't they?

"We'd better get an ambulance," she said in the cool tones of a nurse, "though I'm afraid it's too late."

Steve merely clamped his mouth shut tight and said, "How did she do it?"

"There was an empty bottle. Barbiturates, I guess. Her breath smelled of alcohol. That wouldn't help, would it?"

Steve shook his head.

"I'll see about the ambulance," he said. "Chin . . . get her out of there. Okay?"

"Yeah," Chin answered unhappily.

The girl had walked on.

Chin said, "Better than jail, though?"

"Yeah," Steve said. "Better for *her*."

Somewhere a guitar was strumming "*Aloha Oe.*"

Farewell To You. . . .